Year of the Elephant

A Moroccan Woman's Journey Toward Independence

and other stories

Year of the Elephant

A Moroccan Woman's Journey Toward Independence

and other stories

by Leila Abouzeid

Translation from the Arabic
by Barbara Parmenter

Introduction
by Elizabeth Warnock Fernea

Modern Middle East Literature in Translation Series
Center for Middle Eastern Studies
The University of Texas at Austin
Austin, Texas 78712

Library of Congress Catalog Card Number 89-062509

ISBN 0-292-79603-x

Printed in the United States of America

Cover: Photograph by Heather Taylor
Design by Diane Watts

Editor: Annes McCann-Baker

I dedicate this book to all those women and men who put their lives in danger for the sake of Morocco and did not expect to be rewarded or thanked for it.

Leila Abouzeid

Table of Contents

Preface

This translation would not have been possible without the contributions of three persons to whom I wish to extend my thanks.

First, my friend Elizabeth Fernea, who had the idea for this English edition, and followed it through to the end. Her good insight I discovered when I grew to know her better during my stay at the University of Texas at Austin. I came to understand the reason behind the success of the numerous projects she has previously undertaken, namely her books on the Middle East and North Africa.

I trust, therefore, her decision to promote a translation of *Am Al Fil* into English, and I am confident that the resulting *Year of the Elephant* will meet her expectations. Whatever impact this translation might have in the future is a tribute to her. I thank her also for the time she devoted to reviewing the translation and for the final touches she brought to it.

My thanks go also to Barbara Parmenter, the translator, for her perseverance in devoting her time and good style to this work and for carrying it benevolently through. Barbara did a remarkable work and succeeded to a great extent in rendering in beautiful English the mood, spirit and style of the Arabic.

Annes McCann-Baker, Editor for the Center for Middle Eastern Studies at the University of Texas, is the other person I wish to extend my thanks to, for her enthusiasm, encouragement and efforts to get the book published.

This book appeared in episodes in *Al Mithaq* newspaper in Rabat in 1983. It was first published in Morocco in 1984 by Dar Al Maarif, then in Beirut by Dar Al Afaq Al Jadida in 1987. The short stories were all broadcast by the Arabic service of the BBC, and some of them appeared in numerous newspapers in Morocco.

The main events and characters throughout the whole collection are real. They have surprised or moved me in real life, and I wanted by their reconstitution in this book to provide the same feelings for the reader. It was not until I read the translation that I could have that experience, as I could for the first time look at the book from a distance and see it as a reader.

I have not created these stories. I have simply told them as they are. And, Morocco is full of untold stories. Often, I have looked at faces in the streets and said to myself: If they could write, what wonderful stories they could tell.

Leila Abouzeid

Introduction

The publication of Leila Abouzeid's novella, *The Year of the Elephant: A Moroccan Woman's Journey toward Independence,* and the accompanying collection of experimental short stories is an event in cross-cultural literary history. The first novel by a Moroccan woman to be translated from Arabic to English, a task admirably executed by Barbara Parmenter, it is also one of the first works by *any* Moroccan writer to be translated from Arabic into English.[1]

Modern Moroccan literature has received international attention recently, with the awarding of France's most prestigious literary prize, the Prix Goncourt, to Tahar Ben Jelloun for *La Nuit Sacrèe* (Editions au Seuil 1982). The English edition, *The Sacred Night*, has just been published by Harcourt Brace Jovanovich (1989). Ben Jelloun, however, writes not in Arabic, but in French, as the majority of contemporary North African writers have done until recently. Len Ortzen, whose *North African Writing* (Heinemann, 1970) introduced many modern writers to the English-speaking world for the first time, focuses on nine figures, eight men and one woman, all of whom wrote in French. The only Moroccan writers included were Driss Chraibi and Ahmed Sefroui; the only woman was an Algerian, Assia Djebar.

Tahar Ben Jelloun, who did not appear in Ortzen's pioneering volume, was born in Fez in 1944 and lives now in Paris. His earlier novel, *The Sand Child,* has now appeared in thirteen languages. Early reviews described it as "mythic, symbolic, poetic..." and as "a cynical, dreamlike exploration of the roles into which Arab men and women are shaped." *The Sacred Night* is concerned with the same themes, with "a Morocco of allegory and hallucination, of fairy tale and surreal imagining...of protest and a quest for freedom—from roles, from pos-

---

[1] The exception would be the life histories and stories of Moroccan men, told in Arabic to the American novelist Paul Bowles, and translated by him into English, e.g., Driss Charhadi, *A Life Full of Holes* and Mohammed Mrabet, *Love and a Few Hairs.*

sessions, from hypocrisy and from unhappiness." The earlier Moroccan works translated by Len Ortzen also dealt with the issue of freedom, but those works published in the sixties tended to focus on the struggles for independence from French colonial domination and the aftermath of those struggles, the search for identity, for economic security.

Leila Abouzeid's novel published in the early 1980s is both similar and different from these novels by men. *Year of the Elephant* deals with Morocco's struggle for independence and its aftermath, but through the experience of one working-class woman. And though it is like Ben Jelloun's work about men and women and the roles into which Arab men and women are socialized, the perspective throughout is that of the woman, not the man. The style is more immediate than dreamlike, the tone more ironic than cynical.

The fact that Leila Abouzeid writes in Arabic rather than French is significant. She is actually trilingual, but has chosen to write in Arabic, she states, "for political as well as personal reasons." To understand the impulse that animates her to write in Arabic rather than French, we need to see the novel—and the writer—in historical and cultural context.

Abouzeid was born in 1950 into a middle-class family in El Ksiba, a Middle Atlas village where her father was an interpreter in the French administration. She was six years old when Morocco gained its freedom from France in 1956, a process of resistance in which her own father was involved. Rather than enrolling in a French lycèe like earlier members of Morocco's elite, she attended a Moroccan lycèe, where Arabic as well as French was a major part of the curriculum. She went on to Mohammad V University in Rabat and studied as well at the London School of Journalism. Following her studies, she became a journalist, writing for local Arabic magazines and newspapers. She also served as press assistant in the Ministries of Information and Equipment and in the Prime Minister's Office. She wrote and directed an immensely popular talk show on the national radio network, and was an anchor woman for the newly created Moroccan television channel. In that capacity, she came to understand and know the problems of many Moroccans, male and female, of all classes, of rural as well as urban origin. She is thus a product of independent Morocco, and represents the members of the generation who came to maturity under a new central government, in a society very different from that of their parents. *Year of the Elephant* addresses three inter-related problems of this new generation: the issue of history, the issue of a national language and the issue of feminism.

For Western audiences, the dramatic events of the bitter bloody Algerian revolution have tended to overshadow the particulars of Moroccan nationalism and its impact on the wider Islamic world. But in the Middle East itself, Morocco is seen as having played an important role in the area's nationalist movement. Morocco's experience of colonialism and struggle against colonialism is unique. Morocco was never part of the Ottoman Empire, which ranged from Eastern Europe to Arabia and across North Africa encompassing almost all the countries which are today called Middle Eastern. Morocco's unique history is stressed by social scientists, both Western and Eastern, who point out that until very recently, Morocco consisted of an area of independent but related units. In the cities, a form of central government obtained (*bled el-makhzen*); but in the country, the tribes made their own laws and were termed *bled el-siba* or areas of dissidence. The tribes usually declared an annual allegiance (*bayaa*) to the sultan of the ruling dynasty, a symbolic act which helped reduce inter-tribal conflict, but generally they operated more or less independently. In the seventeenth century Portuguese and British merchant seamen foraged and settled along Morocco's Atlantic coast where pirate incursions were frequent. But no real challenge was posed to the uneasy balance of inland power between *makhzen* and *siba* until the invasion, first of the Spanish, and then the French toward the end of the 19th century.

Some background to the development of Moroccan nationalism is helpful in comprehending the genesis of Leila Abouzeid's novel. The era of Western colonial rule is usually seen by historians as beginning in 1798, when Napoleon invaded Egypt. The French began to settle in Algeria in 1830, but the conquest of Morocco took much longer. In the mid-19th century, the Sherifian Sultan of Morocco was still sending arms and supplies to the Algerian Emir, Abd el Kader, in his continuing resistance to France, even though substantial numbers of French settlers had arrived, taken over and were already cultivating land in Algeria. The Moroccan challenge was too much for the French, who struck back, subduing a Moroccan army on August 1, 1844, at Isly. After this, the Sultan was obliged to withdraw his assistance to the Algerian resistance. In 1860, Spain seized Tetouan, an important city on Morocco's northern Mediterranean coast. Even then, Morocco continued to fight French and Spanish take-over attempts, and it was not until much later that France "pacified" most of the rebellious tribes, made compensatory arrangements in exchange for support with other tribes, and established the protectorate, shared with Spain, that was to last for forty-four years.

But the establishment of the Protectorate, signed and sealed at Fez on March 30, 1912, did not entirely end Moroccan resistance. Resistance actually never stopped. Less than a decade passed before the famous Rif revolt began, under the leadership of a wealthy land-owner, Mohammed Abd al-Karim Khattabi, who was understandably unwilling to have his property appropriated by foreign Europeans. He began by defying the Spanish and then the French in 1921, and eventually became the leader of a large coalition of tribes from the Rif, the mountainous northern tier of Morocco, that battled Spain and France for the next five years. The Rif rebellion, though little noted at the time in Europe and the United States, caught the imagination of the Islamic world, which, since the signing of the 1919 Versailles treaty, had begun to demonstrate against the European powers. That Treaty had been much anticipated by the Arabs, for they had been promised independent statehood by Britain and France in exchange for their support against Germany. But by the terms of the Treaty, those promises were abrogated. Britain, France and Spain literally divided the Ottoman Empire among themselves, creating mandates and protectorates throughout the Middle East and ignoring the pleas of the leaders of countries that had expected freedom. Morocco was one of them.

The continuing Rif revolt helped raise hopes across the area for successful opposition to the European colonial powers. Money was collected for the rebels as far away as India and their success was used by Tunisian nationalists to rally support for their own movement in Tunisia. "A whole mythology grew up among the masses in the cities, centered around the Rifi leader," states C.R. Pennell.[2] After all, small bands of poorly armed tribesmen in the northern Moroccan mountains had inflicted serious military losses on the modern armies of the two most powerful European countries; this was clearly the stuff of mythology and legend, and remained in the memory of the Moroccan people who were to resist later. The name Abd el Krim was often invoked in the events of the 1950's which are the dramatic center of *Year of the Elephant.* Spain alone estimated that 10,000 men were lost in the first years of the revolt, and another whole army nearly perished.

Abd el Krim's son finally surrendered in 1926 and was exiled to the French island colony of Rèunion, but the repercussions of the Rif revolt continued. In 1946, he escaped from Rèunion and settled in Cairo, where until his death in 1963 he was the titular leader of the North African Defense League, the umbrella organization of the Northwest African Nationalists (Pennell, p. 216)

In *Year of the Elephant,* the author has focussed her narrative on the final stage of the battle for an independent Morocco, a stage which, according to scholars of the period, "may be considered as having begun on January 22, 1943, with the meeting at Casablanca/Anfa between President Franklin D. Roosevelt and Sultan Sidi Mohammed ben Youssef."[3] (The United States as a political model became part of that period, the particulars of its Bill of Rights borrowed for inclusion in the nationalist articles and pamphlets championing the right of all peoples to self-determination.)

Leila Abouzeid's novel carries on the cover page the following inscription: "I dedicate this book to all those women and men who put their lives in danger for the sake of Morocco and did not expect to be rewarded or thanked for it." She suggests that the majority of Moroccans were involved in the struggle, including the Sultan himself, who was to become Mohammed V, Morocco's first independent and much beloved

---

[2] *A Country With a Government and a Flag* (Cambridgeshire: Menas Press, 1986).
[3] Stephane Bernard, *The Franco-Moroccan Conflict, 1943-1956* (Yale, 1968 for the Carnegie endowment for International Peace).

monarch. This, too, is in contrast with the experience of other Middle Eastern countries. In Egypt, for example, the royal family collaborated with, indeed was part of the British mandate government. After the Officers Coup of 1952, led by Mohammed Naguib and Gamal Abdul Nasser, King Farouk was forced to abdicate and was exiled from Egypt. The Sultan of Morocco, however, joined forces with the Istiqlal, the major Nationalist party, was exiled by the French for his efforts and thus became a national hero. Leila Abouzeid's protagonist Zahra described this event as follows:

> When they had exiled him, a deep collective grief had fallen over the nation and I mourned with the rest of my compatriots. After that Casablanca had fallen into the hands of demons. We had started to see him in the moon, and in his exile he had come to hold the fate of France in Morocco, as they had said at the time, not the other way around.... Fantastic what effect he had on our hearts! His exile had wrapped him in a sacred cloak, and for his sake the people had joined the resistance, as if he had become an ideal or a principle. Had the French not exiled him, their presence in Morocco would have continued much longer; I'm certain of that. (p. 50)

Historic events animate, but do not dominate this novella. They are the backdrop against which the everyday events of the narrative take place: the childhood and marriage of the woman narrator, the missions of the underground movement in which she plays a part, the final triumph of nationalist forces, the new government in which Zahra's husband is given a post, her divorce and her re-evaluation of what independence actually means.

The 1952 Casablanca Massacre is the event that historians and political scientists see as the turning point in the conflict: The *New York Times'* report of the tragedy, dated December 13, 1952, said cryptically that the number of Moroccan civilians shot down by the French police and army militias was unknown, but numbered at least "several hundreds" (Bernard, p. 100). After this event, support for the nationalists spread to the masses of ordinary Moroccans. Thousands joined the movement, like Leila Abouzeid's protagonist.

The author gives the Moroccan struggle depth in Islamic history by comparing it to an important battle in early Islam, when foreign tribes riding elephants marched on the sanctuary at Mecca. The battle of "Year of the Elephant" was won, not by arms and superior numbers, but by the support of small and unimportant elements: flocks of birds which miraculously appeared and so bombarded the elephants with clay pellets and rocks that the mighty animals were forced to turn back in defeat.

Leila Abouzeid is clearly giving credit to ordinary people for the success of the Moroccan battle of independence; Zahra becomes one of the "flock" of small and unimportant people who made the difference in the undeclared war against French rule: the blacksmiths, the housewives, the spice merchants, the rug merchants, the lorry drivers. To those who in the history books are called simply "demonstrators" or "protestors," the author gives faces and names. We come to know the spice merchant with "a sixth finger like a tumor;" the cheerful blacksmith; the women who hide fugitives in their store-houses; the one-legged veteran of Dien Bien Phu.

The author lets the audience experience important moments through the characters' own reactions. The March 2, 1956 declaration granting Moroccan independence, prepared and announced from Paris, reads as follows:

> The Government of the French Republic and His Majesty, Mohammed V Sultan of Morocco...note that the Treaty of Fez of March 30, 1912, (which had confirmed French rule over Morocco) no longer corresponds to the requirements of modern life and can therefore no longer govern Franco-Moroccan relations... The government of the French Republic solemnly confirms its recog-

nition of the independence of Morocco. (Bernard, p. 349).

Leila Abouzeid passes over the formal declaration; the novel focuses on the King's triumphant return to Morocco.

For the Independence appearance, the Sultan came out on the balcony between his two sons, and the crowds in the Mechouar court raised an incredible roar. People cheered and ululated, laughed and cried...

How many times have I listened to his throne speech delivered that November 18! What a speech! I learned it by heart and can still recite it to this day. Every time I repeat its words, those same feelings of limitless mysticism return, and with them the cadences of the Sultan's voice as he drew out the long vowels. You could hear the people repeating the speech in the streets, even little children.

"On this joyous day God has blessed us twice over. The blessing of return to our most beloved homeland after a long and sorrowful absence, and the blessing of gathering again with people we have so missed and to whom we have been unerringly faithful and who have been faithful to us in turn." (p. 50-51)

The Sultan's speech was delivered in Arabic, the national language of Morocco, but a language which had held second or third class status during the forty years of the colonial protectorate. French, the language of the conqueror, had become the official language, the language of commerce, education, and power. Arabic was relegated to areas of religious affairs, where the classical language was utilized and to the family, where the vernacular, Maghrebi Arabic, was used. Thus it should not come as a surprise as we have noted earlier, that the first modern works of literature written in Morocco and published in the West were written in French, not Arabic, and generally by men rather than women. Far more men than women were educated in the few French schools.

The issue of language and its crucial relationship to identity and power was important even in the years of the French protectorate. Just as the French established schools for their children and a few members of the elite, other members of the Moroccan elite established schools where Arabic was taught, and Arabic became a symbol of resistance. The issue therefore became a major one in the first years of the new nation state. When decisions were made about the future of Morocco, Arabicization of the educational system emerged as a primary goal. It was not simple to implement, however, as Salah Dine Hammoud points out.

> For the few thousand youngsters who were enrolled in school in Morocco in 1955, 80% of their school time was spent either studying French or using it as a medium of learning rudiments of arithmetic, natural science and geography. During the remaining few hours (about 11) in their school week, they were taught the Koran and some basic precepts of Islam as well as some classical Arabic poetry, reading and grammar.[4]

The words "few thousand" are important. The new Moroccan government was faced with a population largely illiterate and untrained, despite years of French educational missions. Although the French asserted that many Moroccans were being educated to assume responsibilities in a modern, changing world, the statistics tell a different story. On the eve of independence in 1955, it has been estimated that in Morocco there were only 40 university graduates, all men, and only six girls who had graduated from secondary school.

The educators in newly independent Morocco had a huge task before them. The Istiqlal Party had promised free education to all Moroccan citizens who wished it, and announced

---

[4] Salah Dine Hammoud, "Arabicization in Morocco: A Case Study in Language Planning and Language Policy Attitudes," unpublished Ph.D. dissertation, University of Texas at Austin, 1982.

their policy of restoring Arabic as the nation's official language. According to Hammoud, "In the 1956-57 school year...in the euphoria of independence, the ruling Istiqlal party, represented by Mohammad Al-Fassi, the first minister of national education, pledged to adopt Arabicization as the language policy, and to immediately implement it in primary schools. The point was that a return to an authentic Arab-Islamic identity had to be at the base of national reconstruction." (Hammoud, p. 40)

The introduction of Arabic as the language of Arab-Islamic identity made perfect sense ideologically, but the proposals met with opposition, some of it based on practical matters. Most of the teachers in Morocco, other than the *faqihs*, or teachers, of the Koranic schools, had been trained in French. Where were Arabic trained teachers to be found? Very few schools had been built by the French. How would the expected large numbers of children be accommodated without the construction of scores of new schools? Curricula at all levels developed under the protectorate were based on the French system; examinations were based on French examinations. How long would it take for new curricula to be developed and who would develop them? Further, many of the officials in the new government had themselves been trained in France or in French schools and had minimal Arabic skills. The second minister of education, Abdelkrim Ben Jelloun, proposed to form an educational compromise: Morocco would become more or less bilingual and the shift to Arabic, seen as a long term goal, would not be as swift nor as drastic as had been envisioned earlier by Al-Fassi, but would take place gradually.

A major argument for the bilingual formula was made by Ahmed Slami, an influential member of the Istiqlal Party. He asked:

> Are we going to Arabize completely, at all levels, train young Moroccans uniquely in the Arabo-Muslim tradition, or institute bilingualism and permit the young Moroccan to have a wide opening onto the world, by the no less solid acquisition of a foreign language; this is

a vital question for Morocco. (Hammoud, p. 43)

This period, when Arabicization and bilingualism were being debated in Moroccan government circles, is the period when Leila Abouzeid herself was in school. She learned both French and Arabic but decided to write in Arabic, not only because she believes it is the proper language of her religious faith and therefore of her country, but because the audience she wishes to reach lives in the wider Arabo-Islamic world, where Arabic, not French or English, is the lingua franca of the majority of the people. She not only writes novels, short stories and reviews in Arabic, but conducted her radio show in Arabic. In addition, she is well known in Morocco for her radio dramatic readings of Arabic classics, and her Arabic screen plays for Moroccan films. She is currently translating *The Autobiography of Malcolm X* into Arabic.

The issue of language use is also related to the role and place of women in Moroccan society. Although a few women received a classical education in Arabic in the Middle Ages, they were always in the minority. Until the 20th century, classical Arabic was largely the province of religion, of law, and primarily of men. Arabic is an example of diglossia, different dialects of the same language being spoken in different contexts. Thus in educated and religious contexts, formal classical Arabic is used; within the home the vernacular is spoken. All this began to change with the end of colonialism and the introduction of Arabic-based education for women and men at all levels. Today, modern standard Arabic is used in the media and newspapers across the Arab world. A similar division existed in medieval Europe, when Latin, the language of the liturgy was restricted to the educated elite, then mostly men. Only when the vernacular began to be accepted as legitimate did modern literature as we think of it today begin to develop, and only then did large numbers of women as well as men begin to write and publish.

Leila Abouzeid writes her novella and short stories in what is called modern standard literary Arabic, but her dialogue is written in a modified vernacular. Hence the Arabic used in this novella is also an important innovation, as Arabic reviews indicate. "I think she has come out with a new style," said the Moroccan author and poet Ahmed Abdeslam Al Bakkali, "a mosaic of expression to describe her old and yet new world." A reviewer in the *Socialist Union* of Casablanca wrote "Through her use of form in *Year of the Elephant*, Leila Abouzeid joins the ranks of modern Arab poets and writers of fiction. Her sentences are short, but they are multi-layered, this opening up to a multitude of interpretations. However, she never loses, in her work, the flavor of classical Arabic." (March 5, 1984) By the time the novella was published in 1983, it had already attracted thousands of readers through the serialization of its chapters in *Al Mithaq al Watani,* a Rabat-based newspaper. Al-Bakkali, on reading these installments, said that "from the very first line, we feel that Leila is holding our hands as though we are old friends, and telling us a story in a simple, enjoyable and attractive style, a style with a high sensibility and great gentleness, the gentleness of an educated, keenly observant woman." The book immediately sold out and was reprinted. The resonances of classical Arabic, the mixture of old and new Arabic present in the novel may not always be apparent to the reader of the translation, but the description of the landscape, the relationship of the person to the land, and the careful, precise images grounded in everyday life, are clear, and as such represent elements found in classical Arabic literature.

Thus *Year of the Elephant* is a new kind of novella, utilizing a new kind of language for a woman in a new independent Morocco. Is it a feminist work? What do we mean by the term? In the West feminism is defined as a movement for granting equal rights to women as well as men. It is also associated with individualism and also with the separation of biology from socialization in determining people's status. Juliette Minces, a French sociologist who writes about Algeria asks, "Can the evolution of the condition of women in the Arab world be evaluated by the same criteria as in the West? Is it not Eurocentric to put forward the lives of western women as the only democratic, just and forward-looking model? I do not think so. the demands of Western feminists seem to me to represent the greatest advance towards the emancipation of women as people."[5] Certainly most people, whatever their cultural and religious background, would agree on certain basic requirements for emancipation: equal rights under the law, for example; equal access to economic wealth and health; protection from various forms of human oppression such as prison, murder, slavery, physical abuse. But within these general bounds, each culture, each woman, surely has the right of choice, the right to form her own "feminist" program using elements from her own and other cultural traditions to fulfill new needs. The final model or ideal of feminism, then, may differ in emphasis, in the pace of implementation, but the goals of justice would be the same.

Year of the Elephant deals with all of these issues. The novel begins with the divorce of Zahra and her sense that she has been treated unjustly.

> I come back to my hometown, feeling shattered and helpless. He had simply sat down and said, "Your papers will be sent to you along with whatever the law provides." My papers? How worthless a woman is if she can be returned with a receipt like some store bought object! How utterly worthless!
> ...Those few seconds destroyed the whole foundation of my being, annihilated everything I trusted. (p.1)

Zahra is then faced with a bleak future, since her husband, her source of livelihood, has discarded her, and the religious law by which her life has been bound has been found inadequate, a further comment on the need for reform of family law which has been expressed in the area since independence.

> "Whatever the law provides." And what is that? Expenses for a hundred days. That shows the extent of the law's regard for women. Throw them out on the street with a hundred days of expenses." (p.11)

---

[5] *The House of Obedience* (London: Zed Press, 1982) p. 25.

What does she do? Whom does she turn to? Her parents are dead in a society where parents are customarily the source of security for children whether they are divorced, widowed or in economic difficulty. She returns to her hometown where she still owns property—one room in a house—her inheritance from her parents. And she goes to visit the religious leader of the local shrine, whom she had known as a child. For a Western feminist reader, this is surprising; women in such trouble would not be expected to go to a religious leader for help. Further, she has been divorced, not because she is independent and difficult, but rather for the opposite reason: she is too traditional. "I don't eat with a fork. I don't speak French. I don't sit with men. I don't go to fancy dinners." (p.9)

But despite such cultural differences, the plight of Zahra is the same as that of a woman in any society who is divorced, illiterate and without economic resources. She must find a way to earn her living, a place to live, a reason to live. This is neither an easy nor a pleasant task. Zahra's life as a small-town daughter, a guerilla fighter and a housewife has not given her any experience she can use in the market place. Her brother-in-law reminds her:

> "These days you need a high school degree to get any work at all. Soon they'll require a college degree, and some day a college degree won't even get you a job sweeping the streets." (p.66)

Although her sister and brother-in-law try to take her in, she refuses with the words, "I'm not anybody's inheritance," a poignant declaration of independence. But the sister persists. "Clearly she expects that like other divorced women I will abide by custom and live with her." (p.65) Zahra rebels: "Do you have legal custody of me?" (p.66) she asks, a retort that she knows will create years of estrangement between her and her sister. But she is determined to make her own way.

By the end of the novel, Zahra has built a new independence within herself, and has lost her earlier bitterness and hostility. She has begun to live a reality which, she tells her old friend, the religious leader "is constituted of work, faith and other things that aren't so important." (p.69)

The novella forces us to ask difficult questions about feminism. What is the relationship between women's political and economic activity and women's independence? What about the relationship of the woman to her kin group? What are the events that force a woman to a new kind of consciousness, a desire for change? What is the role of religion in such change? Is it a force for reform or for reaction? Does true independence imply larger participation, a measure of the world's wealth and happiness? And finally, is Zahra's choice a feminist choice?

The answer to the last question must be both yes and no. Zahra becomes an independent, self-sufficient woman, but in a narrow limited way few feminists East or West would totally accept. And Zahra's experience clearly does not conform to that of most Western feminists. She is not a Western woman, but a Moroccan woman, a Muslim woman who finds comfort in her religious faith. She is the product of a different history, a different expectation. That difference is illuminated by Leila Abouzeid in her successful effort to relate Zahra's independence and the problems associated with that independence to the wider issue of national independence and its problems. One woman's experience becomes a metaphor for society, a view that has less to do with western ideas of individualism than it does with Middle Eastern ideas of the value of the group. The novel does not make an ideological statement, but rather presents in fictional form the real life situation of a real woman, the data that all ideologies must take into account.

Year of the Elephant offers insights into the specific situation of Moroccan women. As the first novel by a Moroccan woman written in Arabic to be translated into English, it suggests new directions within Moroccan literature, the increasing choice of Arabic over French in national writing and the participation of a growing number of educated women as well as men in literary endeavors.

As a woman's perspective on the tumultuous events of recent Moroccan history which led to independence, the novella is unique. No patriotic rhetoric is found here, no self-justification, although there is no doubt that the author takes great pride in the achievements of her country. A certain sense of realism is present, a recognition that there are no easy solutions to the troubles of nations—and peoples.

> In the beginning of the Resistance, we believed the struggle would wash clean all spite and malice, just as we thought that Independence would relieve our cares and heal our sores like miracle cures sold in the market. In fact, we loaded Independence down with a burden it could not bear...(p.67)

Leila Abouzeid's brief novella, in Barbara Parmenter's fine translation, opens a small window through which western readers may glimpse not only an aspect of the realities of Moroccan women's lives, but also an aspect of the rich historical heritage and the complex reality—political, economic, linguistic—that in itself constitutes Morocco in the late 20th century.

Elizabeth Fernea

Austin, Texas
July, 1989

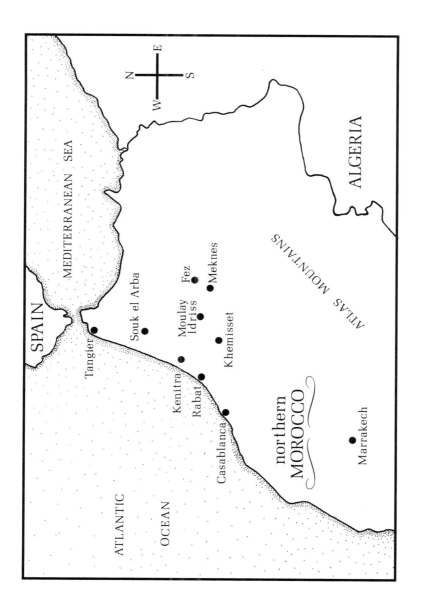

SPAIN

MEDITERRANEAN SEA

ALGERIA

ATLAS MOUNTAINS

Souk el Arba

Fez

Meknes

Moulay
Idriss

Khemisset

Tangier

Kenitra

Rabat

Casablanca

northern
MOROCCO

Marrakech

ATLANTIC

OCEAN

Al Fil (the elephant) is the title of Chapter 105 in the Quran: "In the name of Allah, the compassionate, the merciful. Have you not considered how Allah dealt with the army of the Elephant? Did he not foil their stratagem and send against them flocks of birds which pelted them with clay stones, so that they became like plants cropped by cattle?"

The above is an allusion to a story familiar to the Meccan contemporaries of the Prophet.

> The [foreign] king Abraha, bent on a policy of destroying the power of the Meccan sanctuary, led an expedition against Mecca, hoping to destroy the Kaaba. The expeditionary troops were supported by an elephant (some versions say, more than one). But on arriving at the frontier of the Meccan territory, the elephant kneeled down and refused to advance further towards Mecca, although, when his head was turned in any other direction, he moved. Flights of birds then came and dropped stones on the invading troops, who all died...the birth of the prophet is said to have taken place at this time, in the "Year of the Elephant." And, according to the chronology of the prophet's life, this event would have to be dated in or around 570 A.D.

From the Encyclopedia of Islam, New Edition, edited by B. Lewis, Ch. Pellat and J. Schacht (London: Luzac & Co., 1965) p. 895.

Year of the Elephant

I come back to my hometown feeling shattered and helpless. Yesterday, anxiety was tearing me apart, but today despair is tormenting me even more. I wanted certainty, but when I found it, it only pushed me over the brink into total emptiness. Yesterday seems long ago and life stretches endlessly ahead. Forty years have left me haunted by bitterness. I say forty although it may be more. It seems like a hundred. I have lived without ever clearly seeing the man I married, the man I didn't know until yesterday. And here I am home again, a stranger among strangers. I left just short of my twentieth birthday and haven't been back since my mother died. For whom or for what would I have returned?

This town, my home, had lain buried in my mind like some official document, forgotten until a need for it arose. When he said, "Your papers will be sent to you along with whatever the law provides," I automatically remembered the town.

The other passengers on the bus are getting their things together, absorbed in their own troublesome thoughts. What am I to do now? I've heard of freed prisoners returning to their prisons. Now I understand that, but I feel I can never retrace my steps no matter what fate holds in store for me. Anyway, I'm not afraid and have no desire for revenge. I feel neither sorrow nor hatred, nothing but a vague awareness that something inside me has been extinguished, has finally come to a halt. And yet I have kept sleeping and waking. The soul is the dividing line between the living and the dead. If only I had been torn up by the roots. The thought of death attracts me, but I lack the will to die. Strange how we cling to life!

He had simply sat down and said, "Your papers will be sent to you along with whatever the law provides." My papers? How worthless a woman is if she can be returned with a paper receipt like some store-bought object! How utterly worthless!

Those few seconds destroyed the whole foundation of my being, annihilated everything I trusted. My jaw dropped as I stared at him.

"Why?"

"I haven't got a reason."

He picked up the car keys and walked silently out of the house. I don't remember losing consciousness but I woke up with my body contorted, my hands stretched out like those of a corpse. My mind adjusted slowly, as it had on that long-ago day when I opened the door to a stranger who said with an Algerian accent, "They have locked him up."

It is the worst possible time in my life for such a disaster to strike. My family all lie in their graves in the town cemetery. What am I to do?

From the bus window, I had surveyed the impact of the storm, recognized its ominous signs. Trees lay in the middle of the road amidst the rubble of uprooted shacks. The scene reminded me of the flood seven years ago that had swept away everything and left our town in ruins. What the forces of storm and flood destroy is enough to build entire cities. My heart contracted, knowing that this storm was but a warning of worse to come, but I could not worry about that.

The passengers get off at the town gates and disappear. Only the sound of the wind remains. The old cafe stands empty as it has for some time, its chairs set upside down on the tables. Cold and poverty have conspired against it, but it continues to resist death like the townspeople themselves.

I cross the square, breathing in the smell of the town, a mixture of moist earth and dung, and walk through the gates. In the past I had felt intoxicated every time I passed between these portals, but now as I look beyond the town walls at the dilapidated rooms with their rows of arched windows lining the river bank, I feel nothing. Have I lost my own identity?

The flood has gouged the river bed deeper, but less water flows in it. The sound of the remaining trickle is eerie and forlorn in the bleakness of the town's dirty lanes and peeling walls. There are a few small shops scattered about: a charcoal vendor, a tailor, a grocer with mostly empty shelves. The shops belonging to the Jews stand padlocked and boarded up. They once had schools and synagogues, but when they left, business slumped and prices fell. They traded and sold beer and practiced magic, then emigrated, group after group. Boats carried them away from Tangier, leaving only their ghosts to roam the town.

A figure floods back into my memory, a stout woman of average height, her shoulders covered with a shawl that hangs

down in a broad triangle bordered by tassels like those of a fla-
menco dancer. An image going back thirty or thirty-five years.
The Jewish women would stand leaning against the side of
Rahma's door.

Whenever I used to come into our alley, I would find one of
the Jewish women at Rahma's door. There existed an inviolable
pact between her and these women. She read their fortunes and
they brought her various offerings in exchange, kissing her hand
and blessing her as they left. Probably, the business ceased being profitable long ago and she has withdrawn into the darkness
of her house.

Even if I were to forget everyone else on the street, I would
never forget her. Of her I have vivid memories. From the day I
opened my eyes on the world, I watched her and felt the impression of her grow increasingly stronger in my imagination. She
was a colossal figure, above and beyond anything the mind
could conjure. Her hair was red from frequent henna dyeing, her
head wrapped in a yellow shawl with silk tassels dangling and
glittering at its edges among the wisps of her curls. She had a
loud voice, a brash, impudent manner, and could pummel her
opponents with abuse as easily as a fighter with his fists.

She spent every day on her doorstep, wrapping a blanket
around her legs during cold spells. No one could come down the
alley without informing her of his or her business, and no two
people could stop to converse on any subject without her joining
in. She was a woman unlike any other in town, and her reputa-
tion carried from the plains to the mountains. Her vast mind
stored all sorts of secrets and scandals, ready for use if the tide
turned against her. When Rahma declared war, all the women of
the alley rushed to watch from their doors and roofs, passersby
flocked around, and the whole street took on a carnivallike air.

Nothing upset her except insinuations about her unknown
origins. Who was she? Where had she come from? How did she
get here? In my whole life I never met anyone who knew. That
was one secret she kept and which she'll carry to the grave.

That such questions remained unanswered deepened the
sense of mystery and provided fertile ground for rumors. She
was a sorceress, an informer, she "had a past." God knows the

truth, but such talk wounded her and impelled her to continue on the warpath and spurn any offer of a truce. Thus, from her open door she issued a constant stream of insinuating song which fell on her enemies like spears.

Inspired by the intimations of our parents, we were all convinced that her house possessed a magic room into which she threw mischievous children. Inside that room, we believed, stood casks and large clay jars filled with treasures from the time of King Solomon, and a long tunnel was supposed to lead from the room to the grotto under the town gates and eventually to a terrifying dungeon beneath Meknes.

One day she quarreled with my mother. The two exchanged insults as Rahma sat in her usual position, blocking the door of her house with her massive frame. Shortly thereafter, she abducted my little sister, and watched from her observation post and tapped her cane with slow deliberation as we rushed around the town frantically searching for the girl.

After the abduction incident, this strange woman soared into my imagination on wings with which I was eager to fly. She dazzled me, casting her spell over me and drawing me to her like a moth to light. I vowed to infiltrate her kingdom and the mysteries behind it, and so began to curry the friendship of her daughter. Yes, she had a daughter, younger than I, whom she claimed to be her own, though of course we didn't believe it at all. She was never separated from the girl nor from her cane, and when she walked she would lean alternately on both as she tottered along, pausing for breath now and then, an effort which seemed to stifle and paralyze the whole street.

I made enormous efforts to befriend the girl, so when Rahma finally invited me to play hopscotch with her daughter, I eagerly accepted. She watched us as we began the game and took turns jumping on one foot over the squares which covered the middle of the alley. Some days passed before the relationship became secure enough that I was asked inside the house.

The other children stared after me in amazement as I disappeared through the door. I felt hypnotized by awe and by terror of the unknown, and walked expectantly with a steady step like someone going into a horror movie, knowing what was to come. I surveyed the place with a hasty but comprehensive glance. There were a few casks, several locked doors, a spacious courtyard with a fig tree in the center, and in the tree's trunk a collection of reed dolls sitting on some small cushions.

As enchanting as the dolls were, my attention immediately turned to the locked doors—so suspicious in the gloom and silence—and to what treasures those casks might contain. Suddenly, from behind one of the doors came a noise like someone walking on straw. All my senses tuned into the sound as I pictured bizarre humanlike creatures with hoofs, horns, and tails lurking on the other side. I tried to convince myself that it was just some household animal, a goat perhaps, but my suspicions were too deep to accept such a mundane explanation, so I stuck to my first impression.

The powers of children to fantasize are matched only by their willingness to believe their fantasies. "She'll never grow. With her mother leaning on her like that she'll never grow an inch." So the children said, and I believed them. Yet by the time I left the town for Casablanca, Rahma's daughter had become a graceful, radiant young woman with luxuriant braids hanging down her back and highlighting her beauty.

When I lived in Rabat after independence, I went out on the night of *al-Qadr*[1] to stroll about the old city visiting the tombs of *sheiks* and *imams*. I made my way through a crowd dotted with groups of children who were fasting for the first time. The girls were all dressed up, their small faces so painted that they looked like little dolls wrapped in white cloth. Other youngsters roamed about the city cafes ingratiating themselves with the customers by offers of shoe shines. Still others turned into temporary street hawkers selling candles at shrine entrances, pulling on the sleeve of each visitor until he or she became irritated, then pouncing on the next victim.

Under a long arcade, in the midst of a crowd swarming like an army of ants, I noticed a group of beggars, their songs of praise heard clearly in the din even from a distance. Among them, to my utter amazement, I saw Rahma's daughter, with a baby in her arms. Her head was bowed, her hair covered with dust, her hands more emaciated than any I had ever seen. Suddenly she raised her head and our eyes met. I recoiled in horror, but the surge of bodies pushed me away and I found myself in

---

[1] the night of power, a night during Ramadan.

the courtyard of a shrine. The emaciated hands and the forlorn look remained etched in my mind. What had happened to her? Certainly women today face all kinds of problems, but what could have led to this?

I was paralyzed by confusion and embarrassment, and afraid of coming face to face with her a second time. I stayed in the shrine a long while before working up the courage to leave. When I finally emerged, she was no longer where she had been, nor anywhere in sight. It was unlikely that I'd come across her again in such a mass of people. After that night I looked for her every time I went to the old part of town, but never saw her again.

And now here before me is Rahma's house, halfway up the alley on the right, its ironclad door bolted shut. Has she gone to the next world? And our house, the same as always. We had divided it up among ourselves from the very start, and after we left, tenants rented the rooms. I walk through the front entrance and find all the doors surrounding the courtyard closed to the cold air, just as we used to do at the beginning of autumn.

I knock on the door of my room and rouse its occupant. She recognizes me when I let down my veil, and after some urging, shows me in. The humble condition of the room fills me with similar humility. I search my mind for a way to tell her why I have come but succeed only in prolonging her discomfort. She seems to be preparing herself for the worst, and is not surprised when I finally tell her that I need the room back for myself. She still assumes I am deceiving her in some way, and I have learned long ago that you can't convince someone without an explanation, so I speak plainly and to the point, watching to see how she reacts.

"I've been divorced and have nothing to my name but this room."

Her brow wrinkles as she opens her mouth, then shuts it again. For our people, divorce is a catastrophe, an absolute disaster. Any objection she might raise is shattered with one decisive blow. There is nothing more to add.

"I'll get out."

I mumble my thanks and she urges me to stay for a glass of tea, but I decline. I know what a glass of tea means to a poor woman, and my most urgent concern is to find a place to spend the night. She escorts me to the door, and I move with great difficulty as though I were handicapped in some way.

Mud, dung, ruins, animals, a garbage collector playing the *mizmar* behind his donkey which is loaded down with refuse. A town mired in the depths of history except for the electric lines and the plastic bags everywhere. I reach the small white shrine with the dome on top. My shoes are caked with mud. I wipe them off and carry them inside with me. The *faqih* sits in the corner, keeping warm in front of a brazier. He is as old as our house. As soon as I see him, I feel reassured. I had feared that he, like Rahma, might have passed on. But nothing about him has changed, as if in his world time does not exist. Or perhaps something has changed. His beard seems to have grown whiter. I take his hand and feel its warmth and softness as I kiss it. He doesn't look up. I sit down, lift up the edge of the mat, and slide my shoes underneath it. His body is thin, his turban thick and spotless, his robe white. He possesses that graceful beauty of old age. How old is he? Seventy? Eighty? More? That's what we said during my childhood, during the days of my grandmother. She had been one of his followers, may God have abounding mercy on her soul. She never ceased to praise him and would get so carried away in his presence during the *dhikr* sessions that she'd lose consciousness. When there were no sessions she'd cry and complain. She took me along whenever she visited him, and I always felt a sense of apprehension as we came to the shrine. She would let the wool veil drop from her face, the veil that made our women appear like white tents walking down the alleys. Every time we arrived at the fruit vendor and turned the corner to the shrine, fear crept into my heart, to the point that the two, the vendor and the fear, remained linked in my mind long after I had grown to womanhood.

I gaze at the *sheikh* as he silently recites verses from the Quran. My anxiety is so intense I feel as if I might choke. I can't say what I want to say. Why are words so inadequate? On the wall an old placard displays the name of Allah in large letters. A globe of colored glass hangs decoratively from the ceiling. I listen as the *sheikh* mutters in his provincial Berber accent, which neither his memorization of the Quran nor a lifetime spent in the town has managed to refine.

"'So despondent were they that the earth, for all its vastness and their own souls, seemed to close in upon them.'"[2]

I freeze in amazement at the eloquence of the words. That was what I had been struggling to say, the exact expression, as if the words had me in mind. The *sheikh* falls silent and I speak.

"May I spend the night here...sir?"

I want to call him by name but can't remember it. He looks up at me and I can see on his face the purity of his heart.

"Have you no other place?"

"No place but this. I was divorced today."

His face clouds over and even I feel jolted by the words. Strange how they retain their bite. Feelings of grief and misery rise from my breast and stick in my throat as tears begin rolling down my cheeks.

"Don't cry."

The tears come faster until I am sobbing. I weep for my life and for my alienation in my own town. Then I dry my eyes and wipe my nose.

"Your accent is a local one," the *sheikh* observes. "Don't try to hide it."

It is true, it had stuck to me like the smell of fish. My accent and my room are all that this town has bequeathed to me.

"Then you don't recognize me, sir?"

"Why, no."

"I'm Zahra, Kanza's granddaughter. She was always coming to see you, right up the the time of her death."

His face lights up with joy, but he seems astonished that a person can change to such an extent.

"This is what fate has led to," he says with a resigned sigh.

"This is what independence has led to," I counter.

"But why?" he asks.

Fury rises up inside me and I exclaim bitterly: "I don't eat with a fork. I don't speak French. I don't sit with men. I don't go out to fancy dinners. Is that enough or shall I continue?"

"Those are their standards?"

---

[2]Quran, Repentence, Chapter 9, Verse 118; from *The Koran* translated by N. J. Dawood (Penguin Books, Great Britain, 1967).

8

"I'm nothing but an old coin fit only for the museum shelf. Their positions in society now call for modern women."

He looks as if he were listening to someone who has just returned from Mars.

"Principles are the most fragile of man's possessions," he murmurs. "How easily people forget!"

"Everyone forgets. The nation itself forgets."

"You have nothing?" he asks.

"Nothing but a room in my father's house that should be free soon, and a maintenance allowance for three months and ten days."

"The town is full of your relatives."

"Only distant ones. And I haven't seen them in years, so what's the use? I know what they'll say. 'You've been gone so long we've forgotten you...How do you stand it?...You've hurt us so much...' No, I'm not going to look up any of them."

"Loneliness is a hard thing for a woman in your situation."

"I despise everyone, including myself. There seems to be such a malaise and feebleness permeating everything. What's wrong? Is it a black magic spell?"

"Be careful now. You're walking on dangerous ground."

"But the prophet himself had spells cast on him," I insist.

"May God's prayer and peace be upon him."

"Did you know that?"

"'All magicians shall not prosper however skillful.'"3

"Is it the evil eye at least?"

"Only God knows."

"And God? Does He let one down?"

He looks away as a bead drops down his rosary, and resumes his muttered recitations.

"Why does God permit injustice?" I ask.

He continues under his breath: "Prayers for the prophet dispel sorrows and cleanse the spirit as filth is cleansed from a white robe."

"The country is wallowing in filth!"

"But it is not completely devoid of good. If it were not for that, anger would have consumed us all."

3Quran, Ta Ha, Chapter 20, Verse 69: from *The Koran* translated by N. J. Dawood (Penguin Books, Great Britain, 1967).

"Are we not already consumed? The whole taste of life has spoiled. Misery flows through the air and mingles with our very breath."

"No pain lasts forever."

"Well, I've decided to live with it. Men I know try to cure it with alcohol, but I confront it completely sober."

"So rejoice. Endurance is the mark of faith."

"I'd have lost my mind without it."

"These things will pass and a reward awaits you in the next world."

"And what's in this one? Nothing at all, or hardly anything."

"The one is temporary while the other is truth itself, so let us have faith and praise God."

We cease speaking and he rises and goes out, then returns with a clay bowl filled with water, barley bread, and some black olives wrapped in paper. We eat the bread and the olives in silence. Afterwards, he brings me a mattress and a blanket, bids me good night and leaves.

The efforts of the day have exhausted me. I thought that I fell asleep immediately, but in the morning I remember hearing the sound of rain falling on the grape leaves in the nearby houses, a sound that seems to have come from my childhood.

I remain alone in the shrine until sometime after noon when I venture forth to see the woman. Since the Jews have left, I know she'll have no problem finding another room.

At the entrance to our alley some girls are playing with a rope, and others carrying babies on their backs. Their faces are radiant despite their poverty, and reflect good health, due I surmise to the plenitude of milk. Families here send their cows to the mountains but keep one or two close at hand, consuming some of the milk themselves and giving the rest away, much to the good fortune of poor children like these.

I pause to watch the girls. Their exuberance amazes me, so reminiscent of my own in this alley four decades earlier. If we had known then what awaited us in adulthood, we would have cherished that precious childhood joy. I tremble in fear of what the coming years hold in store for these girls.

"Whatever the law provides!" And what is that? Expenses for a hundred days? That shows the extent of the law's regard for women. Throw them out on the streets with a hundred days of expenses.

The woman's belongings stand in the courtyard of the house. She soon appears with a porter who loads everything on his shoulders and trudges out, his head bent down on his chest. The woman presses the key into my hand and hurries to catch up with him.

I stand looking around my room, so desolate in its emptiness, so oppressively small. But at least it is mine, and I praise God for that.

I return to the *sheikh* to tell him that my room is free."I can't thank you enough for your help."

"Thanks be to God."

I kiss his hand and get up to leave, but he calls out to me.

"Take the blanket...and the mattress."

I want to thank him but can't find the words. In my whole life I have never found myself in such a helpless situation. I put the bundle on my head and walk humbly home through the alleys.

The *sheikh* is a fountain of goodness in an age when even preachers are adulterers and drunkards.

In my room, in my father's house, I spend the second of my hundred nights, counting them as Scheherazade once counted her own.

Chapter Two

Having grown up and become gray-haired, I return to the winter chill and icy water of this town. Everything is gone, every embellishment, even the olive trees. Independence was the one almighty goal, the key to paradise.

I realize now the importance of having kept this room. Something in my subconscious had prevented me from selling it, and anyway women in our town did not sell the property they had inherited. As a people we combined the ways of both peasants and townsfolk, like someone sitting poised on two chairs. The inscriptions, tiles and marble of our houses, mosques and baths reflected our refined urbanity, while our love of the land and nature bespoke our peasant heritage.

In this valley at the foot of the mountains were mulberries, pomegranates, cherry orchards and olive groves. The plain was a narrow patchwork sown with melons, cucumbers and corn. The Atlas mountains towered above us, their slopes honeycombed with waterfalls, lakes and wondrous caverns. Those who knew Granada said our town was similar in its setting and verdure, but here money was harder to come by, for orchards were our one resource. In these orchards, our menfolk sacrificed their lives; indeed, many were killed at night while irrigating. Orchard thieves put us and our Berber mayor through hell, and, though the town prison was full of them, they kept coming.

Yes, we clung to the land as we clung to our birthright property, and from this dual instinct we have gained our skills in agriculture and crafts. A unique blend or perhaps a similar combination exists somewhere else. Only God knows, for other than this town, I know only Fez, Casablanca, Rabat, and of course the villages through which the struggle for independence took me—Moulay Bouchaib, Khemisset, Souk al Arba. How could I forget? Their names are struck in my memory like coins in metal.

No woman sells her property, so tradition dictates. I grew up among such words and deeds, and from my earliest consciousness I remember my grandmother's constant admonition that a woman has nothing but her husband and her property, and that husbands cannot be trusted.

What I say about this town comes from my childhood, for today children go to school, the crafts and orchards are dying out, and many people have left for Rabat and Casablanca. Soon there will be nothing left here for anyone to live on; even the streams have dried up. What happened to this town? They have marginalized it and sentenced it to death, like me.

My father's house seems to crumble under the weight of its inhabitants. It reminds me of a hotel in Fez where I once spent a night. The courtyard is worn down. Someday it will collapse under us and we'll be buried in the cave below. That cave! A world of wonders in my father's mind, like Ali Baba's cave. In it he kept his axes, hoes, and ploughs side by side with his animals. He spent his happiest hours there handling his treasures by the light of an oil lamp.

I never saw him, may God have mercy on him, without a furrow on his brow. If laughter slipped from his mouth, he would rein it in again and scold us as if the fault were ours. When he lost his temper, he would curse my brothers and sisters, but spare me. I was always the favorite, ever since I had gathered olives, albeit reluctantly, in the cold chill of the Atlas which even the grownups could not stand. He favored me also because I didn't live with him, though I probably only realized that later in life. I used to panic at the sound of his voice, I suppose out of solidarity with my siblings, and would not feel safe again until he had gone or I had returned to my grandfather's house.

As for my mother, my feelings are indifferent; towards her I felt neither love nor hate nor anything else, as if she were a mere stranger I had chanced to meet in the street. She had inherited my grandfather's large nose and emaciated body. When I think of her, I see her coming into our alley wrapped in a snow-white, striped covering. She held cleanliness in excessive regard and was tireless in her housework. She sang as she worked, and always her songs were about her enemies. She wore a red bead with a white center in her ear; whenever my grandmother would bring her bundles of embroidered slippers, earrings and linen from Fez, my grandfather would tell her as we looked them over, "May you wear it with joy." To which my grandmother would respond, "May you outwit those who envy you," or "May you blind your enemies," or something of that sort. By this, my grandmother meant my father's sisters and the wives of his brothers. I don't recall when I first understood this exactly, but I am certain that such repetitions made me aware from an early age that my poor mother lived in a nest of snakes.

In any event, my house was in fact my grandfather's house and in it I awoke every morning and thanked God for my life and blessings.

My grandfather was around a hundred years old, maybe more, maybe less, I'm not sure. His teeth had fallen out, but he had grown others. He had come down from the mountains and married my grandmother and settled in the town. He spoke Arabic without an accent. In my mind he was a white shirt split at the shoulder where the cord of his money purse crossed over it, a thick turban, a big nose like a fig, and a white beard.

I raced about, played, did anything I pleased, and no one in his house could touch a hair on my head. My heart poured out with love, and a rosy horizon stretched before me. I was captivated by life. I would stare at the stem of the old grape vine, follow it up to where it intertwined with the parapet of the court-yard, and feel that my joy had no bounds.

When I think about going back home, home for me is the house of my grandfather. But where is it now? His heirs have sold it, and it has been resold since. I am without a home, as if this town is just an airport and I a passenger in transit, with no one even to wave at me. But that cannot concern me.

"She's all yours until she buries you or you bury her." How many times my grandfather had repeated that, whenever my grandmother would begin to tell the story...

"You were born the same year your mother moved to your father's house, and she became so ill, we all busied ourselves with her and forgot about you." (I was a burden from my first day out!) "Then we offered to raise you and she agreed." And that is when my grandfather would interrupt and repeat my father's words, that I was theirs until I buried them or they buried me. My grandmother passed away some time after my grandfather, and it was then that I knew I belonged to no one.

I can still picture her face before me, beaming at me, framed by the dangling silk threads of her head scarf. I loved those threads, for they seemed as much a part of her face as her smile. She wore a broad belt embroidered with silk around her stout body. Her good nature and kindness she dealt out to those around her with unsparing generosity.

These two people led me to a shady oasis to pass my childhood before I set out into the desert of adulthood.

Greenery was always around us there, even in summer, but in spring it reached its prime. My grandfather's garden would then become the setting for our outings and parties. Whenever I think of that garden and spring, the fragrance of roses and fruit trees in bloom fills my nostrils, bringing with it delicate memories of my childhood.

To reach the garden we had to walk down a long path redolent with flowers and bird song, bordered by a hedge whose thorns and leaves hid wild blackberries. Above the hedge hung down green branches of pomegranate, their flowers glowing like live coals. Since childhood I have always preferred the pomegranate over all other trees.

Continuing along the path, we would come to a stream over which my grandfather had built a crude bridge of logs and mud bricks. The sunken garden gate appeared to date back to the days of Adam and groaned like a saw when we opened it. Finally, the garden appeared, first in dappled tones of green, then in an explosion of blooms. From these leaves and flowers I learned the names of different kinds of trees.

I also remember white sheets under the mulberry tree, and someone shaking the branches above. The ripe berries rained down like hail followed by leaves floating more gently to earth. Nearby, we children and women would wait our turns at a swing; when mine came, my grandmother would push me, singing a ditty in which my name kept recurring, and my laughter burst forth like water flowing down a staircase. Then my laughter was unending; now I part my lips but cannot manage even a smile.

In a year I learned how to spin, roll, soak and comb wool and became my grandmother's assistant at the age of eight. At that time she began buying with the money I earned pieces for my trousseau and jewelry for my future needs, every time she went to Fez. We women are armed against calamity from childhood on.

Now I seclude myself in this room. "Contemplation is the wont of the intelligent." Slander and gossip. I know these people. Poverty has imposed the lowest of morals on them. Some of them say, I've heard them say, "She's unsociable, aloof, a miser even with words." They understand nothing. Some women come to visit me, but their merciless gossip about other households nauseates me. I feel disgust rising in me and my stomach tightens. Tired and irritated, I put on my *djellabah* and go out. I trample their conventions in the mud. They'll be saying, "She's got a screw loose somewhere." At worst, I'll be called mad, pure and simple. I'm no longer capable of flattering or showing deference or blushing at the appropriate time, but this inability has given me an amazing strength. If only my tribulations had come earlier in life!

The bastard will never get what he deserves. The papers will arrive with "whatever the law provides." The law provides nothing. I'm like a student who fails after long years of bitter effort and is ignominiously dismissed. What can he do? What can I do? If only I could think of something. But what options are there in a town as dead as this?

Here they are at their brooms again. They never declare a truce. As soon as the sun rises, a fever to clean seizes them. They'd scrub the ceilings if they could. On laundry day, not a rag is spared soap and water. They remind me of my mother.

I suddenly realize that I have yet to visit my dead kinsmen. After listening to the Friday sermon, I buy some bread and dried figs and go to the cemetery. People are milling in and out; there are men selling candles and others reading the Quran. I find the graves of everyone except my grandfather, and after distributing the bread and figs, a guard takes me to his tomb. As I sit before it, a strange peace comes over me. Death seems so alluring in its tranquility, yet people fear it so much. I don't like these built-up tombs. A city for the dead. At a distance I see rooftops inside the town's walls, whitewashed and rectangular like these tombs. Another kind of city, though I don't know what brings the comparison to my mind.

As the sunlight fades I get up to leave. The unexpected sense of serenity cheers me and I want to hold on to it somehow. I take advantage of this momentary vitality, deciding to explore the town. I walk down every lane and alley, past the wood sellers, the grain and cloth markets, the blacksmiths, and my grandfather's house. There I stop and stand a long time, watching as men, women, teenagers and children go inside. Enough people to make up three families at least, all immigrants from the mountains. The public fountain trickles into its basin of ancient tiles. At one time its water flowed more plentifully, and with it we cleaned our house, washed our clothes, soaked our wool, watered our grape vine, and gave drink to our cow. And now it's as if we had never been here.

I forget myself until nightfall. I shouldn't stay too long in these darkened lanes. I move on aimlessly. What few streetlights there are date back to the days of occupation and give off only a dim glow. One lamp for each lane, the bulb topped by a metal disc like a plate or cap, and mounted on the red earthen walls amid sprouting grass. The bridges are the same as always, and probably go back to the time of Idris the First, old dilapidated bridges for pedestrians and livestock. The river looms murky and frightening in the darkness, its gurgling water echoing in the night's silence. A town that goes to sleep with the roosters and surrenders its alleys to prowling cats after the evening prayer.

I must walk and walk and savor this serenity, for I know my anxiety will inevitably return. My wedding procession passed along this street, and ended in that house over there, the house of my bondage for which others envied me. They envied me the bridegroom, too. In those days, being a teacher of French carried some status. I hadn't known him before the engagement; he had seen me at my grandfather's door watching a musical procession pass by, and had sent his parents to ask for my hand, basing his choice on my long hair and dark eyes. His family had proposed many girls to him before me, but he found some fault or other in each: too tall, too short, not plump enough, too many relatives. My father told them, "The girl belongs to her grandfather," and the family decided to marry me off without ever asking for my thoughts. After that, gifts from the prospective groom arrived on every feast day. One day I heard that the wedding was to be the following week and was gripped by fear.

The festivities finally began—preparing my trousseau, making sweets, going to the bath, slaughtering lambs, putting on henna, receiving the groom's presents, leaving for the wedding night. During the seven days of ceremonies I avoided my grandmother and stole from view whenever possible to weep in secret. When I left for my wedding night amidst ululations and wailing, a feeling I had sensed years before came back to me. I had been with my grandmother at the mausoleum of Moulay Idris the Second[1], eating barley bread and black olives when I saw a corpse wrapped in white linen and draped with a black cloth lying on a board. Frightened and nauseous, I continued chewing my food but was unable to swallow. With that same sense of fear and loathing I departed from my grandfather's house. The procession to my nuptial quarters took a long time, and all along the way I felt the taste of olives and barley bread in my mouth. Does the heart know when the traveler takes a wrong path?

After the festivities ended, my mother and grandmother spent days in bed. The elaborateness of our celebrations must have stemmed from our hunger for entertainment.

I passed a year in my inlaws' house without venturing outside even once. Finally, when I still showed no signs of imminent childbirth, I was sent off to make the round of shrines, burn incense, wear charms, and drink various herbal mixtures. I would have drunk poison if they had given it to me. When they gave up hope, their treatment of me worsened considerably. In the face of their unceasing reproaches, I became convinced that I was indeed the guilty party and labored under that burden ever after. I'm not so sure now that it was my fault.

Had he listened to his mother, he would have divorced me then and there. Barrenness provides sufficient grounds in a society uninterested in the true causes of such things. Or he could have married again at least. His mother did not live to savor the sweetness of this victory. Instead, she came to rule my

---

[1] ruler of Morocco towards the end of the ninth century. By the end of his reign virtually the entire population professed the Islamic religion and spoke Arabic.

life like a feudal overlord. I was to wake up every morning and praise her for having given birth to her son. May God never again make us live through such a time.

I'm amazed that I endured that period. If I had had the same thoughts then as I do now, I would have spat in her face, slammed the door, and walked away.

The day he announced that he was being transferred to Casablanca, she struck her face, tore her dress, and accused him of disloyalty and contempt towards his mother. I remembered what my own mother constantly had repeated, that patience brings relief from suffering, and, as I left the town, I felt intoxicated by my emancipation.

Family and neighbors had followed us out beyond the town walls, waving and some wiping tears as our bus departed. The journey took three days as the coal-powered bus jostled along at what in those days we thought was great speed. We changed buses in Fez and again in Rabat, and I experienced for the first time sleeping in a *foundouk*, a two-storied structure with rooms on the second floor opening onto a veranda. A large open space below for mules and horses functioned as the *foundouk* garage. The analogy reminded me of the day my father had bought a small truck to transport grain and olives. The whole town came out to witness the event. My father smiled proudly. "A machine invented by the blue devil!" my grandfather said.

"If only it ate straw," father replied.

Casablanca is a city of whites and blues, the vibrant heart of Morocco, open to all comers. Final destination for masses of migrants and home town for the entire country. Tall buildings, lights, cars. A new world, a fantastic world. An egg incubated by the defeated regiments of occupation only to hatch an uncontrollable demon that grew up quickly to devour its own progenitors. I took days to discover the city. At first it scared me, but I soon came to love it all: the port, the shrine of Sidi Baliout, the shanty town Carrière Centrale, the Ben Msik neighborhood, the boulevards and shops, and the ease of meeting people and making new friends. Good, fertile earth in which every seed grows. I spent ten years there (the stages of my life, it seems, proceed by decades), ten years that molded me into a different woman, with both feet on the ground and my head held high. But I still hadn't learned to say no, until misfortune struck.

What else can I say about those early days in Casablanca? I try to recall but can't think of anything. Days of ease pass so quickly and uneventfully, we hardly take notice. One day seemed much like another, my time divided between caring for the house and caring for myself. Changing jewelry and buying rare fabrics provided my greatest pleasures. The markets of Casablanca enticed me. In those days I was the very model of elegance, the height of fashion, so said one of my mother's friends upon each triumphant return I made to our town, bedecked in rings and earrings. The news would race through town and everyone would rush around, ostensibly to greet me but in fact just to see my jewelry.

Later, the struggle for independence began. That's another story. I happily sold my olive trees, my jewels, everything worth selling for the cause. Resistance took the place of emeralds and rubies in my life, and today I feel only contempt for such trinkets. Thank God our whims and fancies change!

As for the resistance, I don't think I really knew where I stood at the beginning, or did I? My recollection is so foggy on that matter; no one event or image stands out to clarify the picture. Being concerned, even obsessed with myself as the "model of elegance," I must have been heedless of the world beyond. No doubt I was, yet I did take a position years before actually joining the resistance. I remember the day and the occasion quite clearly. The slaughter that black day in Casablanca can never be forgotten. Whenever I think of it, my body goes numb. I see them, soldiers from the Foreign Legion, emerging from a barracks close to our neighborhood, their machine guns blasting down passersby.

How long I lived with those shots reverberating in my ears and the sight of women and children falling constantly in my mind. Later I would see many corpses lying like garbage bags on the sidewalk, but they never affected me like the events of that horrible day. I found myself in an apartment, the owners, features and location of which I didn't know then and still don't today. In the midst of the terror, I lost all awareness and simply reacted as if walking in my sleep.

As the shock wore off, a sense of desolation replaced it, a feeling of all-pervading tragedy like the loss of a loved one, of defiance stifled by impotence. That day I lost all affection for life despite its luster of clothes and jewelry. The situation had to be changed or it was not worth living.

The incident had begun when one of the soldiers from the barracks started to harass a Moroccan woman. A Moroccan man was gunned down, perhaps trying to defend his compatriot. Passersby rushed to the scene, the gathering turned into a demonstration, the demonstration into a bloodbath. Hundreds of defenseless civilians slaughtered in the streets of their own country as the price for a mercenary's lustful whims!

The memories come back hand in hand, but what am I doing in a deserted alley at this late hour of the night? Conscious of my surroundings again, I feel that sickening sensation once more. Shadows are emerging from the mosque in front of me, some of them coughing in the humid breeze. The breath of dawn rises around me, its blue light faintly showing and bathing the town in the smell of morning.

Chapter Three

"Your papers will be sent to you along with whatever the law provides." How shameless people are! Positions of power come to those not yet mature enough to handle them. They have no time or room for growth. They think such positions will last forever, are theirs by eternal right. Someday he will awaken to a reality as bitter as my own and his world will come crashing down around him. Have I been living with an enemy all this time? Were it not for his appointment to that office, I would have died without ever really knowing him.

The papers arrive along with what the law provides. The post office notifies me and I go and wait in two lines, one for the papers and one for the money order.

Is there a greater humiliation in this world? For me there couldn't be. While I am asking for a money order form and filling it in, my sense of bitter resentment overwhelms me and turns into a pounding headache. I had learned to write in those evening classes where we battled illiteracy among those who could neither read nor write, but where the educated learned nothing.

I write in the amount I have received, put down my ex-husband's name and address, and return the form with the money to a postal clerk. A cold fog envelopes me, as if I were living the initial shock all over again. Just as I had walked out of his house a month earlier, I walk out of the post office and feel the same sense of being lost. On a bench in the sun, I sit down. Recovering a bit, I realize where I am—a public garden left by the French. A small troop of children comes by, running and shouting around me. The world is rotting about us, yet people still procreate. Such is human nature!

"Children provide proof that God has not yet despaired of the human race." I don't remember who said that, but if it's true, glory to God whose patience is without limit!

Annoyed by the noise of the children, I return home. The gloom of the day casts a sadness over the house and a chill unrelated to the cold weather seeps through it. I strip off my *djellabah*, roll it into a ball, and sit down. The room has a musty smell like that of old books, and is cramped and dispiriting. It would be better for me to go back outside, but remembering the din of children, I gently lay the *djellabah* beside me. Slaoui on the radio again. Who invented the radio anyway? Sounds of a quarrel filter in from another room. A house that never knows peace. Was that written in my destiny as well?

Putting on the *djellabah* once more, I leave the house and wander aimlessly in town. The public auction is reaching a crescendo amidst circles of buyers in the used goods market. Is it Thursday then? In the cloth market a merchant uses obscene language with two women concealed behind woolen wraps. These markets oppress the spirit. I say that, having expended years of my life in such shops, but now I feel that they have choking iron fingers.

"You were the very model of elegance." So says a neighbor from our old alley. A friend of my mother, she had witnessed my triumphant returns in new outfits, rings, and earrings. As word would spread, townspeople would rush to the house, ostensibly to greet me but in fact wanting to ogle my jewelry. Hopelessness leads to carelessness. I realize that, looking at myself as the woman speaks, but what I see doesn't torment me.

I leave the town, cross the square and walk past the bus station. Some homeless men sit smoking *kif* in the deathly stillness of the cemetery. One breaks a wine bottle on a tombstone. At the sound of shattering glass I spin round and race back towards town. Angry at myself, I head towards the shrine.

Some women are in with the *sheikh* but they soon leave. I crawl near him to speak, my fingers fidgeting with the sleeve of my *djellabah*.

"Things are getting worse, sir."

"Relax and tell me what's happened," he replies with extraordinary calm.

I remain silent until I overcome my tears, then swallow hard. "The papers have arrived."

"Did you not know they would be coming."

"Of course, but..." We fall silent. The voice of a blind man reciting the Quran fills the shrine. As I surrender to the sound of the words, my fear eases and I feel at peace.

"What will become of me?" I ask abruptly.

He remains unruffled and answers quietly, scribbling with his reed pen. "He who believes knows no fear and his heart is not anxious."

"Yes, but I could starve."

"In the land of Islam, no one dies from hunger."

"But I have no means of support."

"There is a carpet factory in town."

"I don't know how to weave."

"Surely you can knit."

"My eyesight is too weak."

"Your spirit will rust if you yield to idleness."

Then I remember. I can spin wool. I report this fact to him as exuberantly as one telling of a gold strike. "You see," he says.

I had forgotten that I could spin wool just as I had forgotten the *sheikh*'s name, just as I forget what day of the week it is, just as I lose my way in the streets. I must pull myself together.

I haven't touched a spindle for twenty-three years. There has been no need, and in the last few years women have thrown their spindles away to join the struggle for Independence.

When had he joined that struggle? I don't know the exact date. The day I found out I was stunned. It was the same shock I felt when he sat down in front of me and said, "Your papers will be sent to you along with whatever the law provides," yet that earlier surprise brought pleasure, even joy, rather than pain.

Throughout his participation I, too, entered the struggle and carried out missions for my homeland. But now what does my homeland do for me.

"The struggle has come to nothing," I say to the *sheikh*.

He stops writing and points his pen at my face. "Deeds followed by remorse do not please God. He does not like those who remind of past favors, either."

"If I had to do it all again I would."

My nationalist activities began by chance one evening with a knock on the apartment door a few minutes before curfew. No doubt whoever it was had good reason to come at such a time. The knocking continued and he opened the door as I stood behind him. The light reflected a bony unshaven face the color of eggplant. Inside the hood of the bulky *djellabah*, that face looked like a clenched fist. My husband stood at the door, nonplussed by the unexpected visit. The man in the *djellabah* pushed him aside and stepped into the hall.

"The woman hasn't come back yet."

I went into the living room and closed the shutters. The men followed, the visitor first. He pulled off his hood and sat down. "I'm giving myself up."

My husband stood leaning on the door frame. I stood by his side. When the siren signalling curfew sounded I switched off the lights and lit a candle. All around us the sound of shutters banging shut rang out like gunfire. Then silence engulfed the street as if it had lost its tongue.

"They came to my wife," the man said. "Allal confessed. He told them how to identify me." He pointed to his knee. I peered down following his finger and glimpsed part of an artificial leg beneath his *djellabah*. I quickly looked away. His arrival had so startled me I hadn't noticed he was crippled. With an anger that seemed to lessen his distress he invoked the days of Dien Bien Phu, spat upon their memory and said, "I gave my leg to France and now it will lead them right to me, a tragedy which nobody will record because it is to us that it is happening. This is my payment for Indo-China."

I kept my gaze fixed in front of me, embarrassed as if I had to answer to him for France.

At that time he said no more, but after Independence he spoke often and in detail of the war, tirelessly repeating his stories. Vietnam was for him still Indo-China and, as he recalled his time there, his features would soften and sadness color his voice. He had two daughters there whom he hadn't seen since the end of the war. Two daughters who were lost to him while fate elected that his wife Roukia be barren. A strange fate that decrees only what should not be.

He continued to correspond with the girls, in French, but when he became engrossed in his Indo-China he spoke only of jungles where the trees twisted and curled around each other, of skies weighed down by smoke, of guns, snakes and explosions, of camps, nurses and doctors, and of the leg on which he was walking as part of a patrol under the command of a Moroccan officer, the leg that was missing when he awoke. He never talked about his daughters, never. But we knew, and he knew we did, and we all went on, skillfully feigning ignorance.

His daughters and the leg were two sores from Indo-China which were still festering in his heart. His daughters who would die Vietnamese without ever seeing the land of their Moroccan ancestors, and that hideous piece of metal on which he walked by day and which lay cold and lifeless apart from him at night. Two wounds that provided incitement enough for his hatred of France and his unending battle against it.

Was that why he joined the resistance? Or was he like us spurred by nationalist feeling alone? I don't know. Frankly, after what happened the night he arrived at our apartment in his coarse wool *djellabah*, and even though I heard him insist many times after Independence, as if he sensed my doubts, that he would have joined the resistance regardless of the leg, I am not truly certain. Although no one ever brought up the events of that awful night, whenever we reminisced with Faqih about the struggle I couldn't keep from thinking about it, and I always felt he knew what was going through my mind.

That night when he said the leg was his payment for Indo-China and I fixed my gaze ahead of me feeling embarrassed, my husband said firmly, "Forget the leg for now."

"I'm in great danger," replied Faqih (I learned his name later.)

"And you leave your hiding place?"

"Someone saw me. A woman neighbor. She started spreading rumors. So the woman asked me to leave. Who can blame her? Her husband's a *fida'i* and already in prison. What would you have done?"

"I know, but if only you could have held out a little longer!"

"I'll tell you plainly, I won't be able to resist. Look at Allal. I thought he'd never break down. Whenever we talked about the situation, he'd go white and stiffen behind the wheel. And when we'd pass colonialists' farms, he'd get so upset we'd nearly run off the road. 'These estates belong to you and me,' he'd always say, 'and look how foreigners profit from them while we spend our lives on the road delivering cartons of soft drinks!' When we decided to destroy their crops and I came to you for directions, I was convinced that, as Allal used to say, I was more entitled to die than the hundreds who were dying every day because I understood better than they what the word 'Morocco' meant. But I'm afraid for the cell. He knows me and I know you."

His voice resonated danger, increasing our own anxiety and leaving us at its mercy. Suddenly we heard someone kicking the door of our building. Had my dead grandfather walked in at that moment I would not have been more frightened. We scurried about the room in confusion. "Where can I hide?" pleaded Faqih. "Under the bed?"

My husband moved toward the door and opened it. Faqih shot by him into the darkness. My husband lunged quickly to grab him. "Where are you going?"

"To the roof!"

"And what about the Senegalese?"

He had forgotten them in his fright. They were Foreign Legion soldiers. I don't know if they were really Senegalese or if the term merely referred to their black skin. In any event, my husband, with an extraordinary presence of mind, remembered that they camped on city roofs at night and thus saved Faqih's life.

Faqih came back in. My husband made his way downstairs, lighting matches. He opened the front door and we listened to the ensuing discussion.

"Who lives in this building?"

"Just me."

"What's your name?"

He told them and someone said, "This isn't right. We want the building across the street." The door slammed and we remained motionless in the dark. I've never in my life witnessed a miracle like that. We walked quietly back into the living room, then heard a thin voice pleading tearfully outside. "I don't know where he is!" We rushed to the closed shutters and jostled each other to see. It was a woman whom they had brought out unveiled. From our observation point we could just make her out amidst their caps. The whole street was silent and it occurred to me that all the shuttered windows were eyes.

"I don't know where he is!"

27

One of them slapped her. "In Maarif[1] you will know," he said in Arabic, pronouncing the "r" with a French accent. "He's at his cousin's." She dropped the information as if it were a live coal she had picked up not knowing what it was. They dragged her to a jeep and sped away. The roar of the engine faded and we could hear children crying in the woman's house. A patrol appeared at the end of the street, and the thud of boots mixed with children's cries.

We walked away from the window in disbelief. What power set that scene at that moment? It was a night of miracles. We sat overcome with amazement until my husband turned to Faqih. "You're going to give yourself up? Eh? Did you see? With a slap on her face she turned in her husband."

Disgust flashed momentarily across his face and Faqih's dark complexion paled. Within the rough wool of his *djellabah* his small head looked like that of a turtle. He spoke as the candle cast his shadow on the wall. "I can't bear up under the whip, I'm warning you." A threat or a plea for help? "I'll confess." Madman. He forgets that the individual dies for the sake of the group just as he earlier forgot the Senegalese. "I'll give them your name...and the name of the woman who hid me."

My husband's look of disgust increased and I sensed that he wanted to throttle Faqih. Instead, he stood staring at him until Faqih broke. It's true that weakness causes rash thoughts. "Find me a way out," Faqih begged, defeated.

"We will."

I spent the night in feverish sleep. When the curfew lifted my husband left the house. He returned and found me at the kitchen sink. "He will travel with you to Souk al-Arba dressed in woman's clothing. Tomorrow is market day. Ask for Rahal the spice merchant. He's tall and thin, wears golf trousers and an eastern-style turban and has a sixth finger like a tumor on his left hand."

I dressed quickly and brought a *djellabah* and veil for Faqih. I found the two of them arranging Faqih's leg. "Rahal will help you get across the border into the Spanish zone tonight." He pulled some bills from his pocket and handed them

---

[1]the central police station in Casablanca

28

to Faqih. We helped him put on the *djellabah* and veil and departed.

My husband bade us farewell as we took our seats on the bus. But the vehicle remained motionless. It would be delayed an hour or two, maybe a day or two. That's how it was in the colonies. People protested. When a man with a roster arrived, a youth called from the back of the bus, "When will you let us go?"

"When God permits," replied the man in a challenging tone, egging the boy on.

"If that's the case, why bother to set a departure time at all?"

This was what I had been fearing. Everyone's eyes were glued on the two, waiting for a fight, the same people who had been so anxious to leave a few minutes earlier. No one cursed Satan to appease the two adversaries until I finally volunteered. It seemed the man had been waiting for this gesture. He pressed the roster to his chest and stepped down from the bus.

"We'll go when we go," a woman said. "What's an hour or two?"

"In that case we still need the colonizers," the youth replied.

The passengers muttered disapprovingly, but no more was said. Attendants pulled up the cover on the left side of the bus. Vendors hawked their goods at the windows with a persistence one couldn't help but admire. The bus finally started rolling, the vendors moving with it as we nosed into traffic outside the station and slowly made our way down the street past barracks, patrols and workers whitewashing over anticolonial graffiti.

Faqih sat next to the window, keenly watching the streets, passersby, shops, everything he could take in from the bus. Clearly, he yearned to be back amidst life and people. After being secluded in a stairwell closet for nearly a month, he found everything tinged with beauty and charm. He had slept and awakened at odd times, spent nights awake fiddling with the radio, switching from station to station; only a cigarette relieved the darkness. As dawn came, he'd watch the room gradually take shape around him, then listen for the sounds of morning filtering in from the street.

When talking later of that period, he never forgot to stress his sharp political instincts. "I heard them announcing a radio program to discover new singers, broadcast all around the country," he always reminded us. "They called it 'Sing, Youth.' Youth singing? When we were trying to get them to take up guns? Thinking about it, I realized their real aim was to distract the nation's young people. My deduction was confirmed the next day when Roukia on her regular visit told me that during the first show a bomb had exploded at the Al-Hambra Cinema in Rabat. I told her I knew that was going to happen. She said they were reporting the bombing as the work of terrorists. 'They call us terrorists,' I said, 'while they are the true core of terrorism.'" Every time he told this story he looked at his wife, delighted with himself. "Isn't that so, Roukia?" She would corroborate it, increasing his delight.

On the bus heading for Souk al-Arba, however, I couldn't see his face under the veil to try and read his thoughts. I knew only that he was fearful for his life. Out of respect for his suffering, I left him to himself and we both withdrew into our own apprehensions; that served only to magnify our distress.

We had gone some way towards Rabat when vineyards began to appear on both sides of the road, the vines laid out in long rows with red earth between. In among the vineyards sat houses with red-tiled roofs. Suddenly the bus slowed and pulled off the road. As the engine stopped, passengers craned their necks or half-stood to see what was happening.

"Engine trouble."

"A search."

"Traffic jam."

I tried to stay calm despite the fear gripping me. Finally, the driver announced over his shoulder that it was a military convoy passing. I let out my breath in relief. Some passengers got out to stretch their legs as lorries passed filled with soldiers armed to the teeth. A man in the bus cursed at them through the window pane.

After the convoy had gone, the driver sounded the horn and passengers reemerged from the vineyards holding clusters of white grapes. We continued our journey passing field after field of tomatoes until we reached the outskirts of Rabat. Riding through the city, I was struck by its cleanliness, the whiteness of its buildings, its green trees and leafy hedges in bloom around houses and government offices. A European Moroccan gem on the Atlantic coast.

I later became better acquainted with the city while delivering leaflets for the resistance. I found it a small and graceful town, with three landmarks that still stand out in my memory: the Mechouar, the river and the old city or medina. The Mechouar was a large open space where weeds grew wild beneath the trees, a favorite place on Fridays when townspeople would come to picnic in the fresh air and watch the royal procession on its way to the mosque. The river in Rabat was distinguished by a pontoon bridge and small buses that, like dung beetles, crawled back and forth all day long between the city and the water's edge, transporting people for a small fare. As for the *medina*, it was then and will always remain concealed inside its walls like a seed, its maze of alleys endlessly emptying one into another.

Rabat fascinated me in those days and I felt intimately bound up with it. I never imagined a day when that bond would be mixed with such pain. In those days I came with leaflets at least once a month, usually leaving the same day but sometimes spending the night at the house of Hajj Ali, a committed nationalist. He was a husky and enduringly cheerful blacksmith whose skill at his craft fueled his happiness and glowed like live coals under the bellows of his forge. His love for his work was matched only by his love for his country. In addition to distributing leaflets and preparing food for detainees in the central prison, I imagine that he performed many other clandestine activities. After Independence they appointed him *caid* in one of the southern provinces, a position given to many of those I knew then, including Faqih, but that story comes later.

In the colonial period, the *caid* was head of a tribe and lived regally. He was a member of the feudal class that controlled people's lives and property in collusion with the protectorate authorities. The latter had hoped in this way to create numerous pockets of diluted power, thereby weakening national unity and frustrating the central government. The *caid* was a distinguished personage, associated in the people's mind with wealth, power, and fear. The word now denotes a position in the Ministry of Interior that is equivalent to the position of mayor, but in the early days of Independence, the title was still surrounded with prestige.

How had it affected Hajj Ali? How had he prepared himself for such an abrupt change of station? The last time we visited him in the south, he was tense and dispirited as if his fairy-tale happiness had died like the fire in his workshop furnace in the old city of Rabat.

Where had his good cheer gone? His energy and determination? On that day I realized that man's spiritual health, like his principles, is a most "fragile possession" as the *sheikh* at the shrine would later say.

We never visited him in the south again, for after the nationalist movement split we found ourselves on opposite sides in the dispute. And so a friendship we had thought would last a lifetime came to an abrupt close when comrades-in-arms became adversaries, and that was the end of it. What a wicked thing is politics! It divides people and accomplishes what even the devil himself cannot. Our parting of ways was inevitable, anyway. People had changed and bonds of brotherhood like those linking us with Hajj Ali's family dissolved.

A year after his appointment we heard that he resigned. The news baffled us; we couldn't imagine why he would do such an unheard-of thing. We lived in Rabat at the time, and, curious, I went to the medina and wandered deep into its alleys. Nearing his shop, I saw its doors open. The steady rhythmic raps of a hammer grew louder as I approached. Inside, Hajj Ali was leaning over an anvil taking turns with his assistant in beating a hot piece of iron. He saw me and came to greet me, wiping his arm across his forehead. I studied him behind his leather apron, his sleeves rolled up and his face moist with sweat. Laughter came gently and sincerely from his heart like that of a husband who returns home after an argument with his wife.

As I gazed at the fire and bellows and flying sparks, the image of a husband reconciled with his wife pressed on my mind. Comparing him that day with our earlier visit in the south, I saw him as a common man uneasy in fine evening clothes, a man who can only breathe freely if dressed in his worn familiar rags. His reconversion from *caid* to blacksmith did not seem to create any difficulties for him; in fact, as he moved confidently around his workshop he was more than ever before a *caid* in the full sense of the word.

Before the bus departed from Rabat, a man with a stubbly beard and handkerchief wrapped round his head climbed on board singing in an ugly voice at the top of his lungs and banging a cymbal. As the engine rumbled to a start, he walked down the aisle collecting coins in the cymbal. Only when we were actually underway did he open the rear door and jump out into the road.

We stopped again in Kenitra where a water vendor sold us drinks from his large brass jug. After Kenitra we entered the Gharb plain and crossed its river, well-known for its yearly floods. Tree-lined farms and orange orchards followed one after another until we arrived in Souk al-Arba. There we left the bus, which with its remaining passengers continued on towards the frontier and Tangier.

Stepping off, we looked around and saw the market in the distance. As we crossed the dusty ground, mule-drawn carts carrying market-goers overtook us. A Land Rover with the Aspro trademark drove through the throng belting out loud music. It was followed by a trail of dust and a crowd of children, hoping to be given the Aspro hats the Land Rover distributed and racing as fast as their legs could carry them. The children ran beside the Land Rover until it reached the market, then ambled slowly back, Aspro caps on their heads, to find us still walking. Inside the market, the sun poured fire, its flames mixed with dust; yet people were going about their business with remarkable enthusiasm, as if heat and dust were the market's main pleasures. What an assortment of characters we found there! A veiled woman selling insecticides with eloquent speeches. I can still picture her clearly in my mind, for I had always thought eloquence and illiteracy incompatible. A sweet-seller pushed his way through the throng shouting "A Moulay Driss,"[2] and another hawker draped in a colored blanket peddled his wares to interested buyers. Walking on, we found ourselves

---

[2]chant to call children to the candy seller

in front of a spice merchant's tent where an elderly woman was buying black beads. The spice merchant wore golf trousers and a turban of shiny yellow silk. "That won't cover the price, mother," he told her, lifting his turban and wiping his bald head with his left hand. Faqih and I both saw its sixth finger and exchanged glances.

The woman handed back the beads. "Listen, Rahal," she said. It was our man. "Eighteen and that's it." He wrapped the beads in paper torn from a school notebook, took the woman's money and turned to us. I beckoned him closer and he bent, stretching his torso over a rack of spices.

"We have been sent to you from Casablanca," I said.

He straightened up. "See that fig tree? Wait for me there."

In the tree's shade we ate our food, enjoying the western breeze and filling our eyes with the market's movement and colors until the sun lowered and the crowds began to disperse.

The market was empty when Rahal appeared behind his mule. We followed him, walking east through harvested fields where bales of straw and disparate piles of wheat were scattered. Carts passed, taking market-goers home, and the world around us took on the soft glow of twilight. The evening stillness echoed the distant bleating of sheep and manifested the majesty of the Creator, dissolving the anxieties of politics. Around us the land extended as if it were an unbounded sea with Faqih, Rahal, myself, and the mule, spirits from another world.

"We've arrived." It was Rahal speaking, detaching me from my meditation and pointing to a white house enclosed by a cactus hedge. Three dust-caked dogs and a group of children came rushing towards us. Rahal ordered the dogs to be quiet and the children to greet us. The children kissed our hands and the dogs stopped barking, lowering their heads as they walked back to the house at the head of our small procession.

The door of the house was wide and its large courtyard dirt-covered, sprinkled with water and surrounded by rooms giving the appearance of shops in the village market. Off to one side was a clay oven and a halter with fodder in it. As we entered, a woman with a baby on her back came to greet us, bowed, stretched her fingertips towards us then touched her lips with them. She helped Rahal unload his mule, then gathered up our *djellabah*s. I watched her taking Faqih's. She showed no surprise, as if this was not the first time she had encountered a man in woman's clothing.

We ate dinner on the roof to escape the heat of the house. The moon lit the night sky and a single star shone. We sat in silence until Rahal spoke. "We'll take our tea when we have Independence. And anyway, it hasn't killed us to do without it." We had forbidden ourselves tea as part of a boycott of French products. Later we formed a committee, Roukia, Safia, my husband and I. When we heard the Friday call to prayer, we opened the holy book in front of us and took the pledge not to drink tea until the French left. We would have observed the boycott in any event, but the ritual served to reassure our hearts.

"So, have we died without it?" asked Rahal.

No, we hadn't. The sky was a quilt of stars. Faqih reclined on a sheepskin staring at oleander blooms and distant trees across the fields, highlighted in the moon's glow. Rahal and I watched him out of the corner of our eyes. "Things will get better," said Rahal. "You'll see."

Silence enveloped us again, broken only by a symphony of crickets in the warm serenity of that great evening. From a distance came the sound of barking, which was answered by Rahal's dogs.

"Foreigners rule my country," Faqih said bitterly, "and I run from one to the other while crickets sing and flowers shimmer in the moonlight."

We said nothing more and what seemed like a long time passed before Rahal stood and we followed suit. We left the house and Rahal brought the mule, helped Faqih to mount, then mounted in front of him and the two men departed. Standing by the cactus hedge, we watched them go, the woman holding her baby on her hip, until they melted into the fields.

The *sheikh* and I walk out of the shrine to find night fallen and rain coming down.

"Do not forget," he says as I am leaving.

"Forget what?" I don't remember that we have agreed on anything.

"Spinning wool," he reminds me.

"Oh, yes, of course."

Leaving him to lock the door of the shrine, I walk slowly through the rain, while around me everyone is either running or seeking shelter from the downpour.

Hajj Ali, Faqih, Rahal, his wife and so many others. Safia, Roukia, Walter. I met them on the long trek to Independence and grew to love them all. What a time that was! A time that will never come again. They all disappeared with the end of colonization. No, that's not entirely true. I saw Hajj Ali; Faqih and Roukia visited me in Rabat, saw how badly my husband behaved and never returned. Now no one asks after me. How could they know? And even if they did know, would they come to see me in this abyss now that they are *sheikhs, caids,* and *pashas.*

That night we stayed on the roof until at dawn we saw Rahal returning. "Faqih has escaped," he told us when he came inside. He looked at his pocketwatch. "He should be in Tangier by now."

Faqih would return to visit Tangier after it once again passed into Moroccan hands, and the customs house at the old border had decayed into a rat-infested ruin. But on the morning that Rahal returned without him, my heart ached and fear hounded me as I made my way to Casablanca alone. To tell it truthfully, I didn't believe he would ever come back. When his wife came to see me, I reassured her. "Don't worry, Roukia, the Sultan will return and the occupation armies will depart." In my own mind, however, I had many doubts.

After that, Roukia and I organized strikes, collected donations, and learned to read and write. And on a day I'll never forget, we burned Pinhas's shop.

On that morning we went out in our black *djellabahs.* In those days, we wore black to mourn the Sultan's exile, waiting for his return when we would dress in white like strutting doves. I carried a straw basket with a bottle of benzene hidden inside. It was our duty to attack the agents of colonialism. We had warned Pinhas, yet he continued to sell cigarettes. We found the Spanish alley crowded with women, buying and selling, and crates of vegetables on the pavement. We stopped in front of a woman selling lettuce and procrastinated in our bargaining. Pinhas was not far away, his hat just showing behind *Le Petit Morocain*. We crossed over to his shop and walked inside. He lowered the newspaper to reveal his bearded face.

"I'd like to see that satchel," Roukia said. He moved the ladder and climbed up to retrieve it. I grabbed the bottle's neck, pulled out its cork, and tipped it over, spilling benzene into the basket. I lit a match, threw the basket in amidst the boxes and bags, and raced out of the shop behind Roukia. Her huge body seemed to pluck itself from the pavement and propel itself forward in a single mass while my own light frame flowed like wind hardly touching the ground at all. We ran a good distance, but a group of girls called to us, "Keep running or they'll catch you!" I turned and saw them pouring after us. One of them caught up and grabbed my *djellabah*'s hood but it tore off in his hand. I stumbled on a large basket, entangling my foot in its handle, and had to continue running with it until I found an alley. In the alley I paused to catch my breath. To the left stood a cart holding bowls and a pot of boiling snails, and behind it a spice shop and a restaurant selling *harira* soup. To the right a door stood slightly ajar. I pushed the door open to let myself in, then locked it behind me. In the courtyard I found a group of women peeling vegetables.

"I'm a guerilla fighter" I told them.

The women quickly gathered around me, hid my *djellabah* and the basket I had dragged in, then took me upstairs. Peering through a window grill, I could see my pursuers, Pinhas among them, with a police dog. They were holding a piece of cloth to the dog's nose—the hood of my *djellabah*. I turned to the women. "I have to leave." They implored me to stay and I returned to the window. The men were blocking the alley as a crowd formed behind them. The dog was trotting in circles, sniffing here and there as if he had lost his mind. His handler cursed and dragged the dog away, the other men following.

"That dog's a fool," I said to the women in disbelief.

"How could the poor dog track anything in the middle of all those smells, snails, *harira*, spices!" repied a woman. We laughed boisterously, drowning out our anxiety.

I dressed in one of their *djellabah*s, left mine with them, and departed. I never saw them again.

Roukia was in the apartment when I returned and we told each other our stories in great excitement. What a woman! Much more capable than her husband, and by far more steady. God sent them both to me to start me on the road to all I accomplished. After I helped burn Pinhas's shop, missions came to me one after another, missions I carried out alone. If my grandmother had returned from the dead and seen me setting shops ablaze, delivering guns, and smuggling men across borders, she would have died a second death. Had all that even been in my own imagination, let alone my grandparents? May God have mercy on them, they prepared me for a different life, but fate made a mockery of their plans.

"No, I won't kill anyone," I told him one evening.

"They've assigned you a new mission. Your last success has proven you're ready." A smile of satisfaction flickered over the darkness of his face.

"What is it?" I asked impatiently.

"Guns," he replied with his customary terseness.

"No, I won't kill anyone."

My words angered him. The smile melted off his face and disgust coated its darkness. "Who said anything about killing?" he said in the same terse tone. "Killing is for men."

"Then we're agreed on that," I said, relaxing.

He kept silent for a long time, waiting for his anger to subside, then took a breath and said affectionately as if to make amends, "They want you to deliver guns to Khemisset."

"That I will do."

He loaded me down with instructions and information, leaving my mind overwhelmed by anxiety. I felt as if I were reliving the day of the fire. I spent the night seeing nothing but the police dog and Pinhas suspended on his ladder and the basket exploding like a bomb. Then I remembered the basket in which I caught my foot and laughed.

"What are you laughing about?" he asked.

My laughter grew louder, piercing the dark. "I'm remembering the day my hood flew off and I entangled my foot in a basket."

"Tomorrow, watch where you put your feet," he replied, not laughing. I said nothing more and passed the remainder of the night praying for success on the next day's mission.

I woke up in the morning with my head burning and the floor swaying beneath me. I fastened my belt, slipped the pistols wrapped in cloth inside my blouse and recalled my grandfather speaking of Asma, who took food to the Prophet Mohammed and to her own father Abu Bakr, when they were hiding from their enemies in a cave during their flight from Mecca to Medina. "She tore her belt in two, fastened one part around herself, tied the other around her provisions, then slipped out of Mecca." He would pause and take a long breath, while I pondered his nose. As he praised the Prophet and commended his companions, my gaze would shift to his beard which swayed as he spoke, its movement slowly lulling me to sleep and casting a fine thin veil over the image of Asma, which would form in my mind while listening to my grandfather's narration.

The comparison shook me and made me realize that the struggle has been the same down through the centuries, in that women, too, have always taken their part in it.

Riding the bus to Khemisset, I felt nauseous, as if I had spent the previous night at a wedding party. I nodded off, woke again, forgetting where I was. I thought Faqih was at my side, and then cursed the devil.

I had arrived in Khemisset and walked a long way when I heard shouting behind me in French. I turned around to see soldiers jumping from a military truck. Have they tracked me down from Casablanca? I touched the pistols, but the soldiers passed by and headed for a French cafe, laughing and yelling.

I let out my breath and continued walking, twice inquiring about the address. As I approached my destination, I spied a large gathering in front of the building and several police cars stopped in the street. I felt for the pistols again, then asked a tattooed woman what was happening. The *fida'yiin* had killed a man, she said, and the police were searching everyone in the area.

Why did they have to kill him on this day at this hour?

I retraced my route, then wandered for awhile, only to find myself back at the scene of the killing. Seeing a cinema, I made my way to it and bought a ticket. I found a seat in the darkened theatre and looked around. To my right sat a boy absorbed in the film. The seat to the left was empty. What if they searched the theatre?

I placed the pistols on the floor and pushed them under the seat with my heel, then left. Outside, the crowd had dispersed, but the corpse still lay shrouded on the street, its head propped up on the sidewalk. I sat and watched from a distance until an ambulance arrived to retrieve the body. The police followed the departing ambulance and I cautiously approached, searching for the address I had been given. It turned out to be a shop selling locally-made mats and rugs. Inside sat a man wearing a turban wrapped Berber style.

"Are you Moha ou Alla?" I asked.

"Yes, that's me."

"I've come to you from Casablanca."

He leaned towards me and whispered, "With three pistols?"

"Yes."

"Where are they?"

"In a safe place."

He left the store and I followed him to a vacant area behind some houses.

"I'll wait for you here," he said.

I returned to the cinema and was shown my seat again. I pulled the bundle out from beneath the chair with my feet. The film ended, the lights came on, and we filed out the exit. I headed to the vacant lot where the man was waiting. He saw me from a distance and came to meet me. I handed him the pistols and walked back to the bus station.

Chapter Four

The used-goods market is jammed as usual. It has always been like that. My mother was one of those who loved it, for buying and selling. Her tastes were quite refined.

I wander around it several times, buying wool and other necessities for spinning. Though I spend all the money I have, I feel as if I have broken my shackles at last. Throwing my head back and seeing nothing but sky, I inhale deeply and thank Allah out loud.

I return home happy but worried that my joy will be short-lived. Yet, sitting down to examine my purchases, I feel a strong bond between myself and these tools of my new trade. When I begin work, I find it intoxicating and I toil away without letup, as if there exists a blood feud between me and my trade.

Where have the grief and despair gone?

But of course nothing lasts forever. Neither actions nor emotions. As if opening the door to find the stranger that morning had happened in a hallucination or a dream or in some time long past. Still I remember feeling suddenly apprehensive. "Don't be afraid," he told me, scaring me even more. "I'm Rachid." His Algerian colleague. "They locked him up this morning."

I stared at him without seeing him. He took my hand and patted it.

"Be a woman."

I had always considered that the most dreadful moment of my life, until that later day when my husband sat before me and said without blinking, "Your papers will be sent to you along with whatever the law provides."

The wretched man. If I had known then I could have spared myself all that grief when he was imprisoned. But of course I didn't know. The apartment filled with visitors while I sat with my head bound up, swaying back and forth in mourning.

They had accused him of organizing a strike. I visited him and couldn't recognize him. His emaciated cheeks looked as if a hammer had beaten them in. Every time I looked at him, I saw the hammer in my head and felt sickened by pain and nausea.

Lord, would we ever forget what France was doing to us?

How quickly we forgot! She rained blow after blow upon our heads, filling between her and us a sea of blood I thought would never be bridged. Never did I imagine diplomatic relations and trade treaties and whole communities of Moroccans laboring in French cities. Who could have believed such a thing? But after Independence, some began saying, "We also wounded them and truly great nations do not dwell on the past."

They passed sentence and transferred him to Al-Adir. I had heard of that prison, but where was it and how to get there? I inquired, then set off with Roukia early one morning. A bus company employee paid for our tickets from his own pocket, telling us when we tried to dissuade him that my husband was paying with days of his life. He later caught up with us on the bus and instructed the driver to drop us at Al-Adir. The other passengers stared at us. "Detainees' wives."

The bus started moving and headed south down the coast, the ocean to our right, fields and pastures to our left. The fields seemed nearly endless. What God has willed! Morocco's granary.

"The Gharb is just the opposite," I said to Roukia. "Full of oranges. Some vegetable fields, but mostly oranges, and black soil."

We came first to Moulay Bouchaib, a small town named for its venerated saint. Beneath its ancient walls, the Oum Rabia flows into the ocean. We stopped in the town square. Departing passengers brought down their luggage from the roof, while those continuing wandered out to buy food, and porters lifted new bags to the roof. The bus pulled out and we were soon passing through fields again, when we came to a sudden halt.

"Those who want the prison," the driver called.

We descended from the bus with several other men and women. The driver's assistant quickly climbed to the roof to pass baskets to a man on the ladder who handed them in turn to those waiting below. I looked around as the bus continued on its way. Nothing but wilderness. The men loaded themselves with all they could carry and proceeded up a secondary road; the women followed, bringing the remaining bags. The road climbed between rows of leafy eucalyptus trees with white-washed trunks. Our small procession stopped several times, women sitting on bags and men squatting in patches of sunlight shining through the leaves.

"Is the prison much further?" I asked each time we rested. "Seven kilometers from the bus stop," they replied.

The road eventually leveled out, and an open stretch of land appeared with the prison visible in the distance.

"The prisoners are still in the fields," the guard at the gate called to us as we approached. "Wait there."

We sat in the shade of trees and performed first our noon and then our afternoon prayers. The prisoners finally emerged from the fields in single file and we rushed to meet them, each calling out the loved one's name, but guards moved to prevent us from reaching them. A book was brought with our names inscribed in it, and we were called one by one to enter a courtyard where we found the detainees squatting behind a white line. A guard instructed us to squat behind a parallel line in front of the prisoner we wished to see.

My husband asked about Faqih and other news, but a guard came and stood over us so we talked only in generalities. I handed the guard the contents of my basket and he passed them to my husband. When he left I asked what to bring next time.

"Don't come until next month," he replied. "There's a problem with accommodations."

"We didn't think of that," Roukia said.

"You'll find a man named Walter behind the prison," my husband instructed. "He's a German guard married to a Moroccan woman from Chtouka."

"A Westerner who will open his house to us?" I asked in disbelief.

"They're not all the same, and this one in particular likes Moroccans."

A whistle blew and a guard came telling him to go in-side. As he departed, he turned around. "Give my greetings to Casablanca."

We all walked out through the prison gate, one woman wiping her tears with a black veil. Behind the building, we found Walter, a stout man of medium height and very fair skinned.

"Si Mohammed's family?" he asked when he saw us.

"Yes." We didn't know how to be cordial and friendly with a man from the West.

"Come with me."

We walked a few steps behind him as he led us through a wheat field. Everything was quiet in the light of the setting sun except for the sound of breezes rustling through the wheat. On the other side of the field chickens pecked the ground in front of two huts.

"Ya Fatna," Walter called in Arabic.

A tall, brown, broad-shouldered woman emerged from one of the huts, preceded by two small girls with braided black hair who wore traditional loose bloomers beneath their dresses.

"Guests." he said.

"They are most welcome," the woman said, turning to greet us. A dog tied to a rope began barking. The woman hushed it in a Doukkali accent and led us into the hut, bending to pass through the low door. She lit a lantern hanging on a pole, clearing a mat and some painted trunks. We took off our *djellabah*s as she spread a rug over the mat and departed, leaving us to contemplate the back of the distant prison, its iron-barred windows fading into the last light of evening.

Fatna returned with a young girl, carrying a slaughtered rooster. The girl dressed it while Fatna lit the clay oven.

A sense of warm familiarity enveloped us. The man came in with his two small daughters in hand and sat down cross-legged, putting one girl on each knee. Watching him, I felt a strange mix of emotions, a new kind of affection tinged with the dregs of years of loathing and misunderstanding. Everything I had heard and seen since childhood only served to confirm my belief that Westerners were an entirely separate species; I even wondered what they ate.

Walter raised his head and I quickly looked away to watch the back of a hen pecking the ground near the door and Fatna's face reflected in the light from the oven fire.

My door opens and in comes a neighbor. "I knew you must be working. You don't usually stay up this late."

This late? She's come to spy on me.

"I've come to tell you we turn off the electricity meter at nine o'clock."

Look how these women think up excuses. I've nearly finished combing the wool, but my mind is beginning to make strange leaps again. The wool doesn't bring the transformation for which I have hoped. That will occur only when I can rein in my thoughts and hold them firmly in hand. But now I have to sleep.

The electricity shuts off and darkness fills the house. My neighbor walks back to her room by candlelight. I feel completely worn out, as though I had just returned from one of those prison visits. The same exhaustion then as now. Thus, I had been relieved when a woman came to inform me that they had transferred my husband to Ghoubila.[1]

I had been at a demonstration held to greet Grand Val. That was what they called him, and they said he was the new Résident Général, rumored to favor Ben Youssef's return and Ben Arafa's dismissal. He looked to be a tall man as he passed in his open white car, dressed in a white jacket with his black hair oiled and combed straight back. The crowd was pressing around his car as if it were a wedding procession.

The next morning Roukia and I went to the prison. They cut open the bread and sugar loaf I had brought, stuck a paper with my husband's name on the basket and placed it on a large plank with other baskets, which was then carried away by two men. We stepped through the prison gate and they wrote our names on a blackboard, adding a number beside each name. After writing the total at the bottom, they led us into a hall divided by two partitions with guards standing in between. The hall was a din of voices rising and mixing between the two dividers. I searched the other side for my husband until I found him. I asked him how he was, but my question was lost in the clamor. I let down my veil and pulled myself against the partition, trying to hear his words.

---

[1] the central prison in Casablanca

"Freedom is close at hand," he said. News of politics would reach him even if he lay trapped at the bottom of the sea. "Isn't that so?"

"It looks like it is," I replied.

He asked me to bring a *djellabah* and veil on my next visit, then asked for news of what was happening. I told him about events in Oued Zem and the Rif and about French leftists taking our side.

"What else?"

"Ben Youssef is on his way to France."

His face lit up and he slapped the partition with his palm. A guard scraped his key on the wire screen. "All talk of politics is forbidden!"

The next time I returned and was standing in line when a woman approached the prison gate and set down her basket of food. A guard ordered her to move away. When she didn't respond quickly enough to his command, he kicked the basket over and oranges rolled into the driveway. The woman collected her spilled pots and departed, cursing France all the while. He called us and we crowded round the gate as they counted. For the first time there seemed to be few guards in sight. Only one counted us and wrote our number on the blackboard. After he went into an office, I saw a man erase the number, then rewrite it, adding one to it.

In the hall the partition doors were open and prisoners mingled freely with visitors for the first time, another sign that control had been relaxed. My husband was smiling. He immediately wanted to know of political news.

"Negotiations have ended and Ben Youssef is on his way," I told him. "He'll arrive on the eighteenth."

His smile broadened. "Where's the djellabah and veil?'

Reaching beneath my djellabah, I pulled the hem of my skirt from where it was tucked into my belt. It fell to the ground, and with it the *djellabah* for my husband. He bent over and picked it up. "We're worried about one of the detainees," he whispered. "They might kill him."

"You're going to smuggle him out of here?"

He didn't answer. He passed through the crowd and disappeared, then returned carrying a prison uniform. I gathered it into my skirt and again tucked it up into my belt, while he quickly pulled down my *djellabah* around me.

I kept that uniform and carried it with me when we moved to Rabat, and even took it that black day when I left the city for my home town.

I found Roukia at my apartment door with the woman who hid Faqih in her house, a woman she introduced as Safia. We were nearing Independence at the time, and she was participating in meetings, collecting donations, fighting illiteracy and the like, but that was all. I embraced her, opened the door and followed them inside. We sat and talked in our *djellabah*s.

"It has been decided that there will be women's meetings in the neighborhood," Roukia said.

"The three of us are responsible for organizing one of the Bouchentouf[2] meetings," added Safia.

We agreed that we'd hold the first meeting at Roukia's house in two days' time; each of us would contact five or more women who would then tell the same number and so we would gather a group.

Our plan worked and at the appointed time women flooded into the house. In the courtyard, Safia and Roukia and I spoke to them. We told them about the delicate phase our country was presently passing through, and about the new Morocco and how we were just beginning the real struggle for development and economic independence, the great *jihad* as the Sultan would later say. We emphasized the nationalist movement's decision that citizens should contribute as much as they could possibly afford. The women's questions went on and on, and we were stunned—they were more aware and knowledgeable about issues than we were.

Roukia was replying to a question concerning how donations were to be used when she glanced at the door and suddenly stopped in mid-sentence. We all turned around to see Faqih standing there, grinning. After a brief silence during which we were too surprised to speak, a woman began ululating. A second joined in and then a third, and soon the whole house was ululating in joy. Women pressed around him to kiss his hand as though he had just returned from pilgrimage.

---

[2] a neighborhood in Casablanca

One by one, the women left until only we three and Faqih remained. He sat and we sat around him. He asked about the meeting's results.

"We are enrolling in literacy centers," I said. "That's the first thing."

"We're organizing our celebrations for November 18th," added Safia.

"And collecting donations for the nationalists," I said.

"I'm treasurer," said Roukia with unconcealed pride.

Faqih's expression changed to a frown, and after a pause he said something the gist of which my husband was to repeat a few days later, and which cast a pall upon our joy. "I accept on one condition. That the treasury does not enter my house."

Was the era of trust and loyalty coming to an end? Could it really be over? Preparations had already been made, indicating that things were changing, and actions swiftly followed. It is true that principles are the most fragile of man's possessions. How right was the *sheikh*!

Roukia replied to Faqih's condition with the same firmness. "I accept your condition. We give receipts, however, except for fifty francs."

He still refused to have any donated goods in his house. I argued that mine was too small, and Safia finally volunteered her house, thus overcoming an obstacle that threatened to ruin the whole operation.

We returned with the first day's donations in the late afternoon. We sat waiting, Roukia holding the bag under her arm, until a representative from the resistance movement arrived. After he took his seat, Roukia opened the bag and emptied its contents into a napkin. We counted the money and gave it to the man, then sorted through the various goods, still in his presence. Brass and silver houseware, jewelry, clothes, some of them quite elegant.

When we finished sorting, Roukia reminded us that it was time for our classes at the literacy center. We took our notebooks and pens and departed. At the entrance to the alley I said, "The last one comes with the evening prayer."

"Your proverbs are always so mysterious," said Roukia.

I explained.

"A woman who lived near my grandmother had a son who was always causing trouble. He spent every day in the street and only came home after evening prayer. So all day long people would come to her and complain about the boy, and immediately after the last complaint she'd hear the call to evening prayer. Then the boy would come and she'd say, 'The last one comes with the evening prayer.' It became a proverb in our town meaning too many problems and worries."

Roukia laughed. "So at our evening prayer, we fight illiteracy."

"All these events frighten me," said Safia. "It seems as if we're living our entire lives in these days."

"We are living the event of Independence," I replied. "Do you understand what it means for a person to live at such a time?"

Safia continued talking as if she wasn't fully aware of what I was saying. "Yet despite that, I feel like my soul is blooming."

"So do I," Roukia and I both said in unison. We laughed at ourselves and the laughter refreshed us.

It was during those days that news reached us of the prisoners' release. At the prison gates we found a whole nation dressed in white. People were gaily laughing and shouting for no particular reason, everyone saying how great was the Almighty's power to bring change. The general awe of divine power heightened when we saw the gate opening and the prisoners coming out one by one. Like a marriage feast it was, only even more joyful.

The festivities of November 18th followed directly thereafter. What to say that could describe that day? The whole of Casablanca became one huge celebration connected by stages and loudspeakers. Songs and performances mingled with speeches, and the aroma of tea being prepared on sidewalks filled the air.

From our own celebration site on the roof of my apartment building we spent the night watching the festivities below, the city floating in lights and thundering deliriously.

We had hardly caught our breath when someone said we were leaving for Rabat. We boarded a bus, Roukia sitting on the engine head waving a flag and shouting slogans all the way to

Rabat. Later when I reminded her, she smiled and said: "We were crazy."

We went to Rabat in a single mass, riding everything that moved on wheels. The journey took hours—how many I have no idea. From where did we get our strength and fervor? How did we spend the journey? How did we all fit into the palace grounds? Again, I don't know. I do remember that I was eager to get there as soon as possible. A strange sensation urged me on. I knew the Sultan. Even though I had seen him only once, I still remembered his face. I had seen him when he returned from France by sea and landed at Casablanca, where tribal horsemen riding on colored saddles came to welcome him. I had stood in the throng that crowded along the route of his procession and waved as he passed. I had glimpsed his face and stored those features in my memory. A great feeling of affection had welled up inside me, as if I had seen a familiar face after a long absence.

When they had exiled him, a deep collective grief had fallen over the nation and I mourned with the rest of my compatriots. After that, Casablanca had fallen into the hands of demons. We had started to see him in the moon, and in his exile he had come to hold the fate of France in Morocco, as they had said at the time, not the other way around.

For the Independence appearance, the Sultan came out on the balcony between his two sons, and the crowd in the Mechouar Court raised an incredible roar. People cheered and ululated, laughed and cried.

Fantastic what effect he had on our hearts! His exile had wrapped him in a sacred cloak, and for his sake the people had joined the resistance, as if he had become an ideal or a principle. Had the French not exiled him, their presence in Morocco would have continued much longer; I'm certain of that. The crown prince spoke briefly on his father's behalf, and the crowd could not stop cheering in delirium.

And what I saw in the Mechouar that day did not compare with what had happened the day of his return from exile.

How many times have I listened to his throne speech delivered that November 18! What a speech! I learned it by heart and can still recite it to this day. Every time I repeat its words, those same feelings of limitless mysticism return, and with them the cadences of the Sultan's voice as he drew out the long vowels. You could hear people repeating the speech in the streets, even little children.

"On this joyous day God has blessed us twice over. The blessing of return to our most beloved homeland after a long and sorrowful absence, and the blessing of gathering again with the people we have so missed and to whom we have been unerringly faithful and who have been faithful to us in turn."

As the Sultan on that Independence appearance waved once more and departed, a frightening tumult of screaming and shoving broke out in one part of the court. I didn't see what happened but heard later that they had found a collaborator, suspected his intentions, and killed him. What had brought him there any way? His death had, probably.

Another killing of a collaborator came to mind, one I had witnessed in detail. With the recollection came the feeling of tragedy that invariably accompanies death. The vision throbbed to life as if it were happening again before my eyes. I had seen a middle-aged man in a turban and gown turn towards his killer, whose tall height, crooked nose, and Tunisian-style fez I remember well. He wore a *djellabah* and stood a short distance from the middle-aged man, pointing a gun the blackness of which stands out in my memory. The incident lasted only a few seconds. The two stood staring at each other to the last moment, determination shining in the gunman's eyes and the shattered look of a hunted animal in the eyes of his victim. The latter's face contracted in terror as the gun went off and he uttered an unrecognizable, inhuman sound before another shot rang out. I didn't see him fall, or at least I don't remember him falling. The gunman walked quietly away and I watched him as he disappeared up a dusty alley between narrow whitewashed walls.

A few days after the Sultan's Independence appearance, they assigned my husband that ill-fated position in Rabat. Before we left we had to dispose of the donated goods Safia was keeping in her apartment. I'll never forget. With one act she tainted the purity of our struggle and extinguished our trust and optimism.

We had spent all day amid piles of housewares and clothes. Present besides the three of us were a representative from the resistance movement and some used-goods dealers.

When the auction ended, we gave the man the money and left. In the street an image flashed in my mind with the intensity of a lightning bolt. It took me aback, as though I'd seen a snake. A silk dress Roukia and I had brought back from one of our rounds. It had not been among the goods we auctioned.

"You look like you've come from a funeral," he said when I arrived home.

I didn't keep him guessing. Safia had helped herself to some of the donations, I told him. He replied with a cryptic question, similar to Faqih's earlier remark. "Have they already started?"

Safia died that day in my heart, the Safia I knew. Now she is just one more of those whom the winds of change have brought.

How shrouded in mystery people are! You never really know them even when you're convinced that you do. After Safia, it was my husband. He tore the roots of trust from my soul, sowing unending wariness and suspicion in their place.

I tell the *sheikh* about Safia and how she shed her skin like a turtle emerging from its shell. His reply I will never forget. "If a turtle leaves its shell it is no longer a turtle and becomes nothing."

A clock begins striking the hour in one of the rooms. I count its strikes. Were it not for prayer, I would be swiftly going mad from sleeplessness. In prayer I find the certainty that God does not forsake us, and prayer becomes a cure for insomnia. When sleep eludes me, as on a night like this, I pray, and unbeknownst to me until morning sleep comes. What a wonderful discovery!

Chapter Five

After selling the wool I have spun, I reckon costs and find I have made only a few francs. My spirits slump. Consumed by pessimism, I set out for the shrine once more.

In the alleys, broad-shouldered young men stand leaning against dilapidated walls. What are they waiting for?

In the shrine the *sheikh* still toils at his writing for the men and women who come to see him.

A dying town is trying to fight off death with hope and miracles.

I greet the *sheikh*. "Wipe that scowl from your face," he chides me.

I unconsciously pass my fingers across my brow. "It's no use, it will only come back again."

He sets down his pen to listen.

"I sold the spun wool," I say, sitting cross-legged in front of him. "But the money I made won't buy me even a shroud."

"Did the spinning not take your mind off the pain?"

"I learned some time ago how to live with pain. Anyway, a spindle can't block out the past. I can't find any peace of mind."

"What are you getting at?"

"I'm leaving."

"You can't escape from yourself by moving somewhere else."

"I've made my decision and that's what I'm going to do. Don't try to dissuade me. I've no future in this town."

"But it's your home."

"A town where I can't afford to eat is not my home."

"So where will you go?"

"Casablanca."

"What will you do there? You've no education."

I feel an urge to mock, not him but myself. "I have a diploma from the literacy campaign, didn't you know?"

He doesn't answer.

"I wasn't given enough time to prepare myself for the future like everyone else," I continue. I am trying to provoke him and not really meaning what I say.

He keeps silent and I goad him again. "Change came, but only for a handful of people."

"You must not allow spite to devour your heart," he finally replies in his customary quiet tone. He never lacks an answer, and since he takes my bait he is responsible for my next assault.

"Isn't it easy to give advice! You can talk all you like because you're not in my place. You don't understand. They've taken to smoking Havana cigars, eating with knives and forks, wearing furs in the heat of summer..."

"Among the believers there are men who have been true to God," he interrupts me, reciting slowly from the Quran. "Some died and others await their end, yielding to no change."

No one knows better than he how to tame my outbursts. It is true. The only hearts which change are those without faith.

These days my husband needs a wife who will offer cigarettes to his guests and help pave the road to the top for him by any means necessary.

He once found me sitting in the sun with the servants. He glared with that look that said he would shoot me had he a gun in his hand. I felt at a loss, followed him upstairs, then came down again and sat poised on the edge of the sofa as if I were in someone else's house. He walked past me, and I followed him into the dining room.

We sat at lunch with the table between us as though I were applying to him for a job. By then we had drifted far apart. A wall had seemed to rise in the intervening space. His face was that of a stranger, unfamiliar to me. The more I looked at him the more distant he became. He ate with a fork and I with my fingers. The sound of his fork hitting the plate stopped and I looked up. Again he was glaring as if he wanted to kill me. I stood up, tipping over my chair which crashed to the floor.

"You don't like me eating with my fingers? It doesn't please you that I sit with the servants? We fought colonialism in their name and now you think like the colonizers!"

I left the table and went upstairs. I heard his car start, its engine screeching as he pulled out into the street.

The situation had reached a stage where there was nothing I could do to put it right. I understood that he felt he could not properly enjoy the fruits of change, that he needed a new woman in every sense of the word, and I guessed that he was preparing for that. However, my deductions remained mere suspicions until the day our driver did not pick me up from the bath house. Later he apologized, saying he had had to take my husband's secretary to the hotel.

"The hotel?" I asked, fearful that I understood only too well.

"Yes, with the typewriter. They've been working there." This man is either a fool himself or trying to fool me. "Never mind then, it's nothing to do with you. It seems the age of secretaries has begun."

I prepared a speech to make his heart bleed when he came home, but he didn't return that night. When I heard his car in the morning, I dashed downstairs to confront him. He walked in and skipped up the steps. I rushed after him.

"Where have you been?"

"At work," he said, continuing upstairs.

"At work in hotels with secretaries?" He stopped, stunned that I knew. "Are they hotels or whorehouses? And what do you do with the bills? Send them to the finance department?"

At the bedroom door he turned around and slapped me. Holding my face with one hand, I pointed at him with the other and shouted with all my strength as if addressing an imaginary crowd. "And we are waiting for reform to come from the likes of these! You're more dangerous than the colonizers!"

It was during that period that Roukia and Faqih came to Rabat. The morning after their arrival I woke exhausted and remembered them. I also realized that he had again spent the night elsewhere. I lingered in bed for a few minutes, then struggled to my feet and dragged myself into the bathroom. Mechanically, I pulled on my headscarf in front of the mirror without bothering to untie its knot; I tucked in the loose hair. The mirror reflected back a face I didn't recognize, a face worn by the tragedy being waged within me. My eyes sank deep behind protruding cheekbones. My once delicated features now made me look sickly and frail.

I sat down to breakfast with Roukia.

"Congratulations on your house," she said.

"A government house," I replied with indifference.

"Are you trying to keep something from me? You know Mohammed bought it for almost nothing."

I swore to her by the food between us that I had no idea government property could be bought for any price, let alone a pittance as she alleged. At that point I didn't care that I was the last to know. She passed me a glass. I took it and set it down again.

"You look as if you haven't slept," she said in a worried tone.

"I feel that something is lying in wait for me," I confessed with all the grief raging within me.

"You're imagining things," she said, trying to make light of my response.

"Can't you see it yourself? He doesn't even come home at night."

She continued to feign ignorance. "Don't you realize what responsibilities he has?"

"I've got proof I'm right, and last night I had another dream."

Now she too sensed danger and her face filled with anxiety. "May it be good, and peaceful, *inshallah*."

"I saw myself at the top of a ladder, trying to climb to my bedroom. The ground lay far below and the ladder didn't reach the room, so I hung suspended between them. I saw a young woman going into the room. She smiled at me like a snake, but since I was hopelessly suspended in midair, there was nothing I could do to stop her."

"And then?"

"The ladder reared like a horse and banged against two opposite walls."

"Did it throw you off?" she asked, now very worried.

"I woke before anything could happen."

We sat in silence as the fear in us increased.

"That is Satan tempting you with wicked thoughts," she said.

56

I cut her off with a gesture of desperation. "We read our dreams to suit our wishes and refuse to see their real meaning. I understand the dream, Roukia, it's perfectly clear."

The fear was becoming unbearable. After thinking the dream over Roukia said, "We must see a fortune-teller at once. Only she can tell us the truth."

...my house. The government house. The first time I had entered it, I felt I was in a dream. I remember well. A sensation similar to what I felt passing through the open spaces of the Gharb with Faqih and Rahal, a strange impression that nothing was real. I felt it again when he took me to see the new house for the first time. He opened a large gate to reveal a lawn with cypress trees distributed here and there, each pruned into a neat geometrical form. At the far end stood a huge mansion. We walked down the drive and I stumbled. Looking down I saw shoots of grass pushing up between the cobblestones. He opened the door and I followed him inside to find a well-furnished entrance hall with a broad staircase descending into its center. The white marble steps highlighted a red carpet running down the middle and fixed in place with brass runners.

The scene took my breath away. I lowered my veil and gazed around me. He pulled my arm, impatient to continue the tour. He pushed open a door.

"The kitchen."

"It looks as large as Allal bus station," I said.

He opened the cabinets, left them hanging and headed out the door.

"Like the vaults of Solomon," I said following him.

We went down another staircase leading to an open courtyard bounded at the back by a wall with a green door at its center. On the left were several rooms. We exchanged looks. "The garage and servants' quarters," he explained.

He opened the green door and we stepped into a beautiful garden of orange and lemon trees surrounding beds of lettuce, carrots and strawberries. It was at that moment that an eerie sensation seized me that none of this was real, not me, not my husband, not the house, not even the end of French rule.

"My God, who forced them to leave all of this?" I said as we walked back to the house.
"We did! We kicked them out!" my husband answered, laughing hysterically, and I joined him.

So here he was then, preparing to do the same to me, and here I was, following Roukia and a servant into the alleys of Rabat's *medina*, on our way to a fortune-teller! Did I really believe all that mumbo jumbo, which drove my mother to her grave?

My father had taken ill while I was still living in the town. I would visit him every afternoon in the suffocating August heat. The empty alleys would swallow me into their depths and I would hear nothing but the rustle of my own garments. Walking through the narrow passageways, I would note the peeling walls exposing stone beneath the wooden shop sheds, water pouring from copper spigots into old basins, and the smell of summer mixed with the aroma of burning oak leaves used to fuel the ovens of the town's bakeries. I had felt an affection for these things since childhood. I would see the lunatic at the door of the great mosque, disturbing my serenity. I would cross a bridge, my heart bleeding for him. They said that witchcraft had caused his madness. I would arrive at my father's house, greeted by its quiet coolness and trickling fountain. Forgetting the lunatic, I would concentrate on preparing for the afternoon's visitors. Later, my husband would come, and we would go at the call for the sunset prayer, unaware of what my mother was secretly plotting.
She brought my father a magician who put all sorts of charms on him and then duped my mother, convincing her that he could double any gold jewelry she had. The poor woman collected her bracelets and earrings, as well as the necklace and belt I kept with her. She bundled everything up and went out into the darkness. The alleys were empty, the shops closed, and the river rumbling deep in its bed, she told us later. The events of that night cripppled her for life.

She said she saw the man in front of the mosque and approached him. She placed her bundle on the ground and, without looking back, immediately entered the mosque to perform the seven *rakaas* in the *mihrab* as he had instructed her. When she emerged, she discovered he had disappeared with the jewelry, and she was struck by paralysis then and there.

From that day on I had nothing but contempt for magicians and for the government that allowed them to tamper with people's minds and property. Never did I imagine a time would come when I'd visit one myself.

The servant was pushing open an old door, and Roukia and I ventured inside. We followed her into a darkened room filled with women and reeking of incense. A space was cleared near the door for us. No one was taking notice of anyone else. Everyone seemed dazed by apprehension. Our turn came and the woman slowly arranged her cards.

"The fog is thick," she began, "and there is smell of betrayal. Yet we knew how to act like men when it was necessary. They want to throw us to the dogs. Don't despair. Relief is near and those who remain steadfast shall reap a reward."

She had struck directly at my inner wound and I burst into tears. We left as she called for the next client, each of us repeating her words and trying to unravel their meaning.

I concluded naively that the problem would somehow be solved and that relief, as the woman said, was on its way. Yet that same evening, when I very politely asked the maid to bring me something, my husband glared at me in disgust. He sneered in Roukia's and Faqih's presence, "Next you'll be begging her, for God's sake."

What could I do? I couldn't address the servants as if they were beneath me. I wasn't used to talking like that.

"You'd be better going back to a hut," he spat out, blinded by fury, and walked out of the room.

I felt I had suddenly lost all blood from my veins. "You mean your father's hut?" I screamed, making sure he could hear.

Faqih and Roukia decided to leave despite the late hour. Angry and confused, Faqih spoke even faster than usual as he said goodbye. "He no longer respects anyone," he said to me.

"There's no place for us here," Roukia added.

That was the first and last time they visited us after Independence. And I asked "why?" and he said that he had no reason. How could I ask such a question? Well, disasters can weaken minds just as they can sharpen personalities and transform characters.

So I left with nothing but the clothes I had on, and the old prison uniform in a bundle under my arm. I headed for the bus station.

"My papers and whatever the law provides." The bastard. I was enveloped in fog and the ground swayed beneath me. There was a lump in my throat and so much grief in my chest, but in my head nothing, as if it had simply ceased functioning. Only my temples throbbed with pain. If only the pain could stop. If only the lump could pass. If only peace could return.

After that, depression came and abided with me for a long time.

I wandered round and round the administrative district like a bee. With extreme effort I tried to get a grip on myself, to watch where I was going and pay attention, but I could not. When I saw the walls of Chellah[1] I realized I was walking in the wrong direction. I sat on a low wall until I noticed a taxi driving by. I flagged it down and rode to the station.

I don't know how long I wandered lost in those streets nor how I bought a ticket, found the bus and got a seat, nor even when we left. I became conscious when the bus was crossing the Bou Regreg River, leaving behind Rabat and its ancient minaret. I felt I was returning to some past time, living the past over again, that nothing had changed. And for me at least, what had changed?

At Fez I boarded another bus bound for another station. I had spent my life riding from station to station. My body ached with fever and exhaustion, as though I was coming down with a cold.

During the journey home, I became more conscious of my surroundings. I saw the damage done by the storm, and the ravaged scene on top of everything else served to make my depression still more acute.

---

[1] an ancient castle fortress outside of Rabat

"Can I entrust you with renting my room for me?" I ask the *sheikh*, as I visit him for the last time.

"And with anything else," he replies.

"There's nothing besides that and saying goodbye."

He calls on God to grant me the means of licit living, and I implore Him to bless me with good health, for with my age and situation nothing could be worse than ill health. I also pray that with His light He will banish the darkness that has accumulated around me.

For the second time I leave my town, but on this occasion there is no one to wave goodbye. Inside, I am terribly confused, but Casablanca doesn't frighten me. A firm determination impells me to shake off the dust and start anew.

The golden leaves which bestow the enchantment of autumn on our region have fallen, and the trees stand naked under lashes of winter winds and rains. Soon snow will fall and the trees will assume strange shapes in the white vastness like works of modern sculpture.

Rain beats down on the bus and clouds thicken in the gloom.

Fez is the same. Its river, mules and sombre walls. But now its roads are asphalted and there are high apartment buildings, and one can get to Casablanca in a single day.

The weather clears after the rain. Yellow rays pour down on the moist earth and in the light blue sky a scattering of white clouds float like clips of clean wool.

Khemisset. A refueling stop for vehicles and a chance for travellers to buy food and coffee. It hasn't changed, its main street still full of cafes. I see the cinema and Moha ou Alla's shop and my heart jumps. I get off the bus and inhale fresh air, its chill reviving me.

Rabat. My mood darkens when I see it. While we are stopped, I feel I am suffocating. Will I forever associate this lovely city with inconsolable grief?

Three stations, three landmarks. Why has my path passed through them again?

Casablanca. There is nothing like Casablanca. It never fails to cheer me, as if it is smiling and embracing all those ill-fated like myself. I feel emotion rise within me, and I know I want to settle in this city.

I descend from the bus and quickly leave the station. I have no luggage for which to wait, nothing but the prison uniform in the bundle under my arm.

Roukia opens the door. Her face lights up briefly until she realizes something is wrong and her pleasure disappears from her face. I cross the courtyard to a room and sit down. She sits facing me, her worry mounting. I speak quickly to end her suspense.

"He divorced me three months ago and I have no way of making a living back home."

She pales as I speak and begins wiping away tears. I comfort her, saying it isn't the end of the world, but then find myself joining in her tears. Faqih comes in. The sight of our bowed heads warns him something has happened and his worry shows on his face as he greets me.

"Did you know I have been appointed *caid*?" he asks, looking for something positive to say.

Roukia breaks my news to him, and now it is his turn to bow his head. I feel a wicked urge to attack the change from which they are both so clearly benefitting. "Let me congratulate you," I say. "It seems everyone's being appointed *caid* these days."

"Everything will be put right," Roukia says, trying to get us back to the heart of the matter.

"I must find a job, and the sooner the better," I answer to keep her from bringing up the idea of going back to my husband.

"No, that can never be," she replies and as is his custom, Faqih agrees with her.

"I have no desire to argue and no one knows what is best for me better than I do."

"Don't get upset," Faqih says.

"I'm not upset," I say, swatting violently at a fly.

I see Roukia bite her lip and we stay quiet for a time.

"I did well by choosing to be *caid* in Azilal," Faqih says, breaking the silence. "Isn't that true, Roukia? 'Why not Kénitra?' they ask me. What would I do in Kénitra? At least in

Azilal one can enjoy some advantages. I tell them I want it for health reasons but I don't think they believe me."

Roukia says nothing, and Faqih goes on. "There one has plenty of eggs and chickens. It's the country, you know."

"When are you planning to move?" I ask

"Faqih's going first, then I'll join him," Roukia replies. "Don't wait for my sake."

"We decided that before you came," she says quickly before he can speak.

Faqih starts to speak, but checks himself. After a brief pause, he smiles victoriously. "Azilal is a great place to be *caid*," he says. He takes a packet of *kif* from his pocket.

"Where is Azilal?" I ask.

He packs the *kif* carefully into a small pipe which looks like a thimble, lights it and sucks in, making the *kif* burn like a live coal. "It's in the heart of the Atlas," he says, smoke emerging from his nostrils and mouth. "Great climate, great scenery." He kisses his fingertips. "Exactly like Switzerland."

Smoke seems on the verge of coming out of his ears as well when Roukia, mirroring my own thoughts, says, "You'd better stop doing that stuff or they'll drag your name through the mud."

"Soon he'll be smoking European pipes and cigars," I add. He laughs, a hacking laugh more like a cough. "What a hellish thought!" He leaves the room, placing all his weight on his good leg.

"Nothing surprises me any more," Roukia says. "He decided he wanted to drive and if it hadn't been for my stubbornness, which you know well, he would have gone through with it. Can you imagine? Driving with his bad leg?"

"Independence has played tricks with their heads."

We fall silent for a moment and I think about what to do.

"Don't worry," she says.

"I'll never find a job."

"We used to say colonialism would never end."

"If only the future could be easier than the present."

"How many times have we worried about things that never happened?"

"All this because I'm a woman."

"Misfortune doesn't discriminate."

"I mean our return to the shadow after all that has happened."

"They say the chameleon changes color when it's in danger, but afterward it reverts to its true color."

I look at her face and am struck by its flow of maternal warmth. It shows in her movements and in her voice as well, and is particularly evident when she is with Faqih.

She pats my thigh affectionately. "Never mind, it was all for the sake of God."

"At least the nation lives in dignity. I am sincere when I say that. Believe me."

"I know. In a situation like yours one has to be sincere."

Soon after that Faqih leaves for Azilal. An official car comes to collect him and he rides off in fine theatrical fashion.

Roukia goes with me to an olive oil factory to look for a job. The guard asks us what we want.

"The director, please."

"Do you have an appointment?"

"No."

"Why do you want to see him?"

"For work."

"You both want jobs?"

"No, just me."

"Have you ever worked in oils before?"

"No."

He rubs his head. "We have no jobs available," he says arrogantly, as if his father were the owner.

"Let us in."

"No."

"No one treats the poor more hatefully than the poor themselves," I say, furious at him. A car pulls up and he lifts the barrier to let it pass, then quickly sets it down again. I wait for the noise of the engine to fade. "We'll never prosper with the likes of you among us."

"He interrogated us as if he were the Minister of Industry!" Roukia says.

I feel depressed nearly to the point of giving up. We take a bus to another factory. In the same tone of indifference, we are told that we have to make an application in writing.

On the bus I explain to Roukia that, clearly, secretaries and office boys are running the country, but she is afraid to comment on my political criticism.

We finally have letters of application typed by a public scribe and deposit them in a post box.

News about what had happened to me filtered up and down the street; everybody seems to know everything about my life, including my search for a job. One day one of my sisters arrives with her husband. Somebody had passed the news on to her. What could she want? Clearly, she expects that like other divorced women I will abide by custom and live with her.

"Let me take care of it and I'll make him see the stars at noon," her husband says as he comes inside. The fox. He's never stepped in to solve anything in his whole life. A wicked fox, my mother used to call him.

"How could you let us hear the news from strangers?" his wife asks. "Are we sisters or enemies?"

Her husband returns to his original idea. "Let me file a complaint against him."

"What for?" I say sharply. "I've received everything to which the law entitles me. What would I sue him for?"

"Let's at least see a lawyer."

"I don't want anything from him."

Roukia comes in, stopping to arrange their shoes at the door. After she greets them, my sister turns to me. "Get your things."

Me go live with them? At my age have my brother-in-law support me? No, that would never happen.

"Why?" Roukia asks her.

"She's coming with us."

"I'm not going with anybody," I reply.

"Am I not your sister and more entitled?" she says looking at me but obviously intending it for Roukia's ears.

"You have a family and have no reason to drag yourself from one place to another," her husband adds.

Roukia slips from the room to leave us alone.

"I'm not anyone's inheritance," I say more sharply, "and I'm not leaving Casablanca."

"Casablanca?" she says. "Is that what your father left you?"

"He didn't leave me anything, God have mercy on his soul."

For a moment I keep quiet, then tell her I have written to some factories about work and am awaiting replies. Her husband shrugs his shoulders in disdain. "These days you need a high school degree to get any work at all. Soon they'll require a college degree, and some day soon a college degree won't even get you a job sweeping streets."

"I just want a job that will earn me an honorable living, I don't care what it is. I'm not looking for a government position."

"What job could you do at your age?" my sister asks, refusing to concede defeat, as usual.

I have said earlier that I no longer have it in my power to be deferential, coy and cajoling, and when I feel pressured I explode no matter who's responsible. And that's exactly what happens at that moment. "Do you have legal custody of me?" I ask, knowing her response in advance.

My words strike her like a slap on the face. She pales, jumps to her feet and heads for the door, her husband in tow. Outside the door they stop to put on their shoes, still furious. When Roukia tries to persuade them to stay, my sister swears great oaths that she will not, and with some difficulty extricates herself from Roukia's grasp.

Those words spoken in a moment of anger will cost me years of estrangement from my sister. She's like that. Her beauty spoiled and destroyed her. Since childhood it lent her a privileged status and allowed her to do as she pleased, and if anyone blocked her path she declared a feud that continued for years. She imagined that no one was more deserving of love, honor and respect than herself, and if she found someone who was she would begin to slowly destroy him or her.

Fate sent her a man of her own kind and in a horrible way theirs was a perfect match. The day her beauty fades, as it is bound to do, and she no longer commands respect and deference, is the day she will turn into a hideous creature, burning all she touches. If discord creeps between her and her husband, God forbid, the day of judgment will be at hand.

At this moment I have trampled on her wishes, the first time I have done so, though she frequently had done the same to me when we were younger, and still can, presumably. My situation, as I have said, frees me from normal social obligations to cajole, defer, and blush at the proper moment.

I won't see her for six or seven years, and know that I may never see her again. So it is. I tell myself she probably came to Roukia's only to lord it over me, not out of any concern for my welfare. For nothing is more hateful to her than others surpassing her, even if they share the same mother and father.

In the beginning of the Resistance, we believed the struggle would wash away all spite and malice, just as we thought that Independence would relieve our cares and heal our sores like miracle cures sold in the market. In fact, we loaded Independence down with a burden it could not bear, and now we are besieged day and night by new struggles in the world—Palestine, Vietnam, Kashmir, Biafra. How many others are to come?

A woman tells me that the French Cultural Center is looking for a cleaning woman. I don't like the idea and decline, saying I am waiting for an answer from the factories to which I have written. But no answer comes and finally I realize there will be no reply, and then I come face to face with the basic fact that we can't do without the French after all. So I go with the woman.

The French people look at my papers, ask about my past, my age, my health, social situation and other things I don't remember, then say, "We accept you."

I start the job and rent a room. Roukia leaves for Azilal and I begin purchasing used furniture piece by piece.

I never look up any of the other people I have known, but nonetheless learn over the years what the winds of change have brought them.

Hajj Ali is still in his workshop. A man who joined the struggle when it needed him, but who knew how to return to where he belonged. His sons and daughters grew up: one became an engineer and another a university professor. Whenever I think of him, I realize with renewed admiration, as if discovering it for the first time, that from his blacksmith shop he served his country and educated his children.

Rahal is a *caid* in the Hauz.

Walter lives outside Taroudant on a small nationalized farm. Perhaps he's managing it for the government, I don't know. I heard that his two daughters married Moroccans.

Safia's husband was appointed to an administrative job somewhere. Independence changed her, disfigured her, as it did others. She cut her hair and started going out in Western clothes. When I talked of women wearing furs in summer heat, it was Safia I had in mind. The day she stole that traditional silk dress from the donations was the last day I saw her. I can still see that dress quite clearly in my mind. I left Casablanca then without saying goodbye and never saw her again.

Oh, I forgot Rachid, the Algerian my husband worked with and who came with the news of his arrest. Do you remember him? He went back to Algeria where he was appointed to an important office.

Have I left anyone out? The *sheikh* at the shrine. He is as lively as ever and seems never to age. I see him once a year when I return to our town to collect the rent on my room. I often tease him about his sprightliness. "Where do you get it from?" I ask, as others ask: "Where did you get that from?"[2]

"I eat only barley bread, olives and pure water," he says.

"You must be hiding some secret."

"It is peace...with oneself. Nothing else," he says, smiling. He is pleased by the spiritual change I have undergone.

"Yes," I say, reading his thoughts, "my depression and despair have gone, as if they were never there."

"And your hostility to the world?"

"The world is transitory. Must I tell you that?"

"Have you forgotten the past?"

"What's past is an illusion. The truth is found in living reality."

"And what is your reality?"

"Work, faith, and other things that aren't so important. The important thing is that I remember God and concentrate on this idea of mine that we are only passing through this life to build a road to the next one."

---

[2]a cliché used in Morocco concerning officials who became rich after Independence through obscure means

The *sheikh* is pleased and smiles again. "How did you come to this idea?"

"In steps. Do you remember years ago when I went back to Casablanca? I thought my situation was unique until I found a magazine belonging to an employeee at the French Cultural Center. The cover showed a color photograph of a middle-aged man and a beautiful young woman. I was really taken with her beauty. The woman whose magazine it was laughed and said, 'So you're interested in Dr. Barnaard?'

"'Who is he?' I asked

"'The South African heart surgeon who's been in the news.'

"'Who is the woman?'

"'His new wife. He lived with the first one twenty years, then divorced her when he started gaining fame as a surgeon.' I listened with more interest as she continued. 'Now the first wife has written a book telling the story of a woman whose life is turned upside down when her husband's position in society changes.'

"I felt at a loss for words. She took the magazine, leafed through its pages, then returned it to me to show a photograph of the first wife with her son and daughter. Looking at them filled me with sadness. How alike people are. And how I understood that woman! No one could understand her better than I. As if I was looking at myself, as if God creates many copies from one mold.

"'Maybe she was a traditional woman, too,' I found myself saying.

"'Too?' the French woman asked.

"'I mean there might be others like her, perhaps here in Casablanca.' She laughed but I remained captivated by the thought of God's hidden omnipotence. Since that day my preoccupation with my affliction has lessened and I have begun to live with it and get used to it, just as people learn to live with an unforeseen physical handicap. Now I simply work and return to my room every evening and live in the reality of the present."

As I told the *Sheikh*, I have forgotten the past. Completely forgotten it as if it never happened or had nothing to do with me. Nothing but vague, pale memories remain of my depression, and of the year of luxury I have no recollection at all. I call it the year of luxury in comparison with the year of the elephant, that year at the time of the Prophet.

I want to be content despite my regression. I want to believe that life is not full of the wicked alone, and that everything is new and different and as good as it can be.

A House in the Woods

In a small village in the Middle Atlas, the spring sun shone through tall pines, evergreen and dusky as olive trees. Patches of light flickered on the dry pine needles blanketing the forest floor. A small stream gurgled serenely through the trees, flowing over smooth pebbles whose contours were magnified by the water's clarity.

Next to the brook stood three girls who filled the woods with their young voices. From the similarity of their features and dress, they appeared to be sisters. The eldest, about seven, sharp and full of energy, took charge.

"I'm building a house," she said in a commanding tone, "and you two will bring the stones."

She showed them a sample specimen and the two younger girls began hauling pebbles up from the stream and carrying them to the chosen site. They moved back and forth like two ants, while their older sister busied herself with her building tasks. From time to time a pebble would displease her and she would fling it away in disgust.

"But there are no more of the right size," the two little ones would plead in their defense. They nevertheless continued their efforts. When the house was well underway, the two young sisters came up with an idea to make their labors more efficient. The older waded into the stream, searching with great care and concentration for the valuable pebbles and bursting with laughter every time she found one. The younger girl gathered up her skirt to form a sack and followed in her sister's footsteps, catching the dripping stones the older girl tossed back to her.

"You're going to get your clothes wet," a husky voice called.

It was an old man whose dark wool *djellabah* made him difficult to distinguish from the tree on which he leaned. In his posture and dress he seemed an outgrowth of the trunk and its rough bark, and one couldn't tell where the man began and the trunk ended.

The child, absorbed in her work, paid no attention.

"Didn't you hear me?" the man called again.

It was clear that she hadn't heard, so he emptied a small cloth sack of oranges, and walked over to her. He took the pebbles from her skirt, put them in the sack, then gently placed the sack in her hand. She continued her work, scarcely aware of his presence.

He returned to his place, lay down on his back and stretched his arms and legs as far as he could. Inhaling deeply, he luxuriated in the warm fragrance of spring blended with the aroma of resin oozing from tree trunks. A marvelously crafted bird's nest caught his eye as it swayed on a branch in the breeze, fixed in its place as if it had grown with the tree.

"Glory to God, the Supreme, the Almighty!" he whispered. He was mesmerized by the serenity of the place and its pleasant atmosphere. The girls' voices and the birds' warbling came to him in his slumber as if from a distance and lulled his senses.

The little girls were finishing their building. "Now we have to collect flowers to decorate the house," the eldest announced.

As they set off on this new task, the youngest girl noticed a hornet zigzagging up and down. Its movement fascinated her and she stopped to watch, convinced that it was dancing to the beat of its own humming. Seeing it light on a flower, she drew close, bent over the blossom and pounced, only to find the flower in her hand.

"I almost caught it," she said, vexed at her failure.

The hornet continued its dancing and humming in and out of the flowers, and finally disappeared into the leaves of a weeping willow tree.

The two older sisters returned loaded down with flowers and pine cones. The youngest trailed behind, empty-handed and anticipating a rebuke. The three sat inside the house walls, demarcated by pebbles, and began vigorously shaking the pine cones to dislodge their tasty seeds. Seeing the sleeping man, the youngest girl thought of a tempting new game. She took up a long dry pine needle and assiduously pricked his nose. He wrinkled his nose like a sleepy rabbit. Finally roused, he sat up thundering and threatening, and with strength fortified by anger he tore up a small palm sprouting next to him. Waking more fully, his anger subsided. He sat chewing the end of the palm branch until he felt it time to leave. He offered the builders his oranges.

In their exuberance at devouring the oranges, the children trampled on their house. They headed home in company with the man. As their voices gradually grew distant, quiet again embraced the woods. The sunlight faded, the gurgle of the brook grew more distinct. The house lay in ruins amid scattered pebbles and twisted wilted flowers.

A Vacation

The June sun clung to the sky's edge. Its glow cooled and faded until one could stare directly into it, a red disc lighting the fields of grain. A serene calm, disturbed only by the rustle of the wheat, enveloped the world. From a distance, the sound of singing echoed in the quiet air, growing louder as a group of school girls approached.

The group grew smaller as each child in turn headed for home, until only one girl remained.

The last girl hurried home, humming. But as she rushed inside, the melody suddenly stuck in her throat.

"Greet your cousin," her mother said.

The girl reluctantly walked over and gave her cousin a cool kiss. She sat down. Neither child said a word. They listened to the sound of the tea being poured and watched the mother's movement as she unwrapped a loaf of bread and served tea.

When the mother carried the tea tray back to the kitchen, her daughter followed.

"Who brought her here and when is she leaving?" the child asked.

"So much hatred between two young girls!" her mother replied angrily. "You'd think you were fighting over an inheritance. May God punish whoever created school holidays!"

The girl spun around and stalked out of the room. She sat on the front doorstep, throwing stones at the chickens in the yard. She stayed there until darkness fell, the night sounds echoing around her. She returned to find her mother serving tea and bread once more.

In the evenings, she usually listened to her mother reminisce and tell stories, and during these sessions she had learned her mother's history. Her father remained a distant figure about whom she knew little other than that he always spent evenings in the village.

"Did you lock the door?" her mother asked her as she did every night

The girl nodded.

74

"God alone protects us," she added, "not the door."

This remark worried the guest. "Aren't you afraid?" she asked after a pause.

"Ask Roukia," the mother answered. "She's the one who gets up in the dark to let her father in."

Roukia puffed up like a turkey. "Do you remember the time the thieves came inside?" she asked her mother.

"Roukia's the one who first discovered they were in the house," her mother said.

Roukia took up the tale, looking at her mother but intending the words for her cousin. "I was waiting for Father to return, listening for his knock, when I heard rustling in the courtyard. I thought it was someone walking on the dried grape leaves. I peeked out the door and saw a match lit and moving towards me. I shouted 'Hussein!' as loud as I could, so loud I shattered the darkness and made my own hair stand on end. The match went out, then someone scurried off and all I heard was the wind brushing through the trees."

Her mother handed her a glass of tea. She fumbled in trying to replace the lid on the sugar bowl. It clattered to the ground, giving them all a start.

"But did Hussein hear you?" the guest asked after they had recovered themselves.

The mother roared with laughter. "What Hussein? That's Roukia's imaginiation. There was no Hussein."

"But I did hear someone say 'Coming,'" Roukia insisted.

Night had nearly passed when a knock came at the door. Roukia opened it to let her father in, then locked it and hurried back to bed. Everyone slept but the guest. She lay in bed gripped with fear. Pulling the blanket tightly over her head she recited "The Throne" from the Quran.

In the morning the mother instructed her daughter to take her cousin and collect some thyme in the fields. The two girls left in silence. Halfway to their destination, Roukia realized she had forgotten to bring a sack and headed back home, followed by her cousin. To open the cellar door under the house, she took the handle from its accustomed hole in the wall. The cousin stood in the middle of the cellar, while Roukia rummaged around, looking for a sack. Suddenly, the cellar door slammed shut. The girls jumped at the noise, then heard the handle fall on the ground outside. Darkness and silence enveloped them.

Roukia moved slowly along the wall dragging her feet until she found the door. But without the handle how could she open it? She looked through the keyhole at the steps leading up to ground level and listened carefully but heard only her breathing. She banged her fist on the door and called through the keyhole. No one responded. She sat down on the floor with her back against the door to catch her breath. Then she tried to jimmy the lock with her hairpin until her fingers were stiff with pain. She sat again and quickly thought through the situation. It occurred to her that if she could find a piece of iron and wedge it between the door and its frame she might be able to break the lock. She began feeling her way through the dark cellar looking for an appropriate tool when she stumbled over a soft body which grabbed at her leg, uttering a stifled noise halfway between a moan and a pant, like someone trying in vain to scream during a nightmare.

Roukia fell yelling to the ground and kept yelling until she realized that moaning body was her cousin. Even then she continued to clamor, joined by the guest, their shrillness increasing and terrifying them even more. The whole cellar reverberated with a horrific din. But not a sound reached the outside. The cellar might have been a sound-proofed radio studio in wartime.

The terror finally passed and the girls' screaming abated, replaced by sobs and panting that gradually slowed and faded. If a light had been lit at that moment it would have revealed two small girls pale as corpses and shaking like dry leaves in the wind.

As the crisis subsided, both girls entertained the same thought: Roukia, the heroine of yesterday is now confronting the reality of today. This idea gave the guest secret pleasure and perhaps she even smiled in the darkness at her cousin's predicament. Roukia, on the other hand, felt her pride deeply wounded, a pain even harder to bear than being locked in the cellar. In a single moment she had lost all her dignity.

Was her courage an hallucination? A dream? She was seized with doubts. "May thyme never grow again!" she shouted.

Still possessed by fury, she searched for something to occupy her mind. An image of a demon rose to the surface of her memory. On cold nights Roukia had heard the demon's story related by her mother beside whom she would snuggle beneath a wool blanket, struggling in vain to stay awake. Her eyes would close in sleep with the demon's image looming in her mind. This image, however, came to life whenever her behavior grew too rambunctious.

On those occasions her grandmother would send Roukia's uncle to fetch the demon, and it would come into the house swaying to and fro in an awesome ceremonious entrance. It had a black face, she remembered well, and a large head with horns. Hair covered its body and it spoke in a thick husky voice.

Roukia would run to her grandmother seeking protection, her knees trembling and her heart pounding so hard it seemed as though it would burst from her chest. Her grandmother would mediate with the monster on Roukia's behalf, finally convincing it to make an amicable departure.

To this day she had never understood why her uncle locked the cellar door behind him as he went to fetch the demon, nor why it took so long for the demon to appear. And when the monster *did* emerge, her uncle could not be found; when the demon left, it also locked the door and another long wait ensued before her uncle reemerged. The memory so gripped her that she thought she felt the demon breathing in her ear, paralyzing her with fear.

Meanwhile the guest was becoming extremely hungry. She went to the door and tried to pull it open by squeezing her fingers into the crack but she could only catch the edge with her fingertips. She pressed hard against it to consolidate her hold, then pulled with all her strength, only to have her fingers slip out. The door remained firmly closed.

Hunger impelled the visitor into a ravenous search for food. She stumbled against a cask, removed the rag covering it and plunged her hand inside only to find a slippery liquid she recognized as olive oil. She wiped her hand on the rag, dropped the rag on the floor and continued to forage.

Bumping into a pile of sacks, she tried unsuccessfully to loosen the palm fronds with which they were bound. She did, however, locate a small hole in one sack which she enlarged enough to pull out some chick peas. Since her efforts had finally been crowned with victory, she sighed with satisfaction.

Lying on the floor exhausted by her labors, she began her meal of chick peas. How one slipped and lodged in her nostril she didn't know. She immediately sat up and blew her nose, but the pea refused to budge. Filled with fear and not knowing what to do, she called out for Roukia. Roukia fumbled her way through the dark until she brushed against her quietly sobbing cousin.

"What's the matter?"

"A chick pea's stuck in my nose."

Roukia passed her fingers along her cousin's nose until she felt the pea. "A tree's going to grow in your nose," she warned her. "Don't you believe me? Our teacher told us that man is made of earth. And there is a story about a garden that grew on a camel's back. Didn't you hear it?"

The guest's fear increased. "Who wants to hear your story?" she said.

"You're the one who called *me*," replied Roukia. The guest pounced on her like a furious cat and they wrestled in the dark until their strength finally gave out. The battle over, they fell to the floor. A frightening silence descended, broken only by the cousin lamenting her misfortune in a frail, tearful voice.

Suddenly the door opened and a flashlight bathed the room blinding their eyes.

"Oh, you wretched girls!" a woman exclaimed. The girls heard her set a metal coal pail on the ground. "We've turned the place inside out looking for you," she continued. "We searched everywhere. We even sent out the village crier. And you were here all along!"

She forgot about the coal she had come to fetch and took the two girls outside. Their clothes were torn, their hair a mess, and their faces streaked with tears. Night had fallen and they clung tightly to the woman's hands, shielding their eyes from the light as though they were nocturnal birds. They found the house crowded with visitors and Roukia's mother, her face swollen from crying.

"Here they are, here they are, I found them," the woman announced as she brought the girls inside.

"Roukia, are you trying to kill your mother?"

Food was brought to the girls, still in their miserable state. Roukia's father arrived, intending to beat his daughter, but the women intervened to protect her. The chick pea problem then presented itself and suggestions filled the air until the father lost his temper.

"Let me have her," he said. "I'm taking her to the hospital."

The guest's face paled.

"Never mind, I'll handle it," a woman said quickly.

They sat the girl down in front of the woman and watched as she took from her pocket a small box filled with powder. Putting some powder on the back of her hand, she instructed the girl to inhale through her nose.

"Sneezing powder?" another woman asked, and the others burst into laughter. The girl cringed, but the woman sternly insisted she inhale. The girl reluctantly obliged and immediately started to sneeze repeatedly. The chick pea was forced out of her nose, and the women laughed again. But the little girl sobbed and tearfully asked to go home.

"Collect her clothes," Roukia's father told his wife. "We'll send her back on the first bus."

The Discontented

The official left the meeting room. In the hall one of the custodians walked towards him and stopped. The official stared at the familiar face before him. The two men embraced, each asking how the other was and blaming one another for first breaking off the ties of kinship.

"Let's go to your house," the official said. They quickly departed in his luxury sedan. The official again inquired about his cousin's news.

"My pay is very low," he replied. "The children are endlessly in need of things, costs keep rising, and no one gives a damn about us."

"If only you hadn't left school," the official said, a note of censure in his voice.

"It was bad luck," the custodian answered bitterly. He scowled. A long silence ensued. The official realized his mistake and regretted his sharp words. The custodian, staring straight ahead through the car's windshield, muttered to himself. "Fortune, my cousin, lifted you to high office and dragged me to the ground, though you were once as wretched as the rest of us."

They came to the outskirts of town where the government had built housing for poor families. Directed by the custodian, the official stopped his car in front of a small house.

Inside, the official sat cross-legged in silence while the custodian surreptitiously observed him. Despite his fine suit, he seemed at home in the house. He looked down, where through holes in the worn mat, the cement floor appeared. He was perspiring in the heat and sluggish air.

Outside, beyond the open door, lay a large vacant lot full of trash and the remnants of ruined shacks.

Children ran in, one after another. Swarming about him, they seemed to the official to be more numerous than they actually were. The small room spun around him in confusion.

"I wish the house were more suitable to your higher station," the official heard his cousin say after another long silence. He did not know how to respond for he knew the poorer man was comparing their two lives. The custodian busied himself with pouring tea into inexpensive glasses.

"Some people are doomed to menial work," he said as he finished.

"All work is honorable and never menial," the official replied, feeling uncomfortable.

The custodian pulled nervously on his thick moustache with his thumb and index finger, then pursed his lips.

"I'll find you a better job," the official said in a conciliatory tone.

He stood up to leave. Outside more children surrounded his car, and scurried away at his approach. As he opened the car door, he saw that they had scratched "Long live Morocco" on it with a sharp tool. Before leaving he gave his address to his cousin and suggested he contact him again.

Urged on by his wife, the custodian finally arranged to visit the official. But when he arrived at the latter's house, he felt intimidated by its grandeur. A European-style edifice in the middle of a green lawn, it was surrounded by rose beds and slender willow trees. He hesitated, then pressed the doorbell, and for a moment heard nothing in the deep silence but his own breathing. A servant opened the door and showed him into a spacious parlor containing an unimaginable assortment of furniture and objects. Dazzled, he gazed around the room, that first impression settling permanently in his mind. He wondered what sort of wood was on the walls, where the rugs and housewares had come from, and how much it had all cost. Realizing that the roses in the glass vases were the only things with which he was familiar, he sneered inwardly at his own incredible ignorance.

The official greeted him and invited him to take a seat. He had found his cousin a job as a supervisor on a government farm outside Casablanca.

A supervisor? A government farm? Casablanca?

"But I know nothing about farming," he stammered.

"You have only to oversee operations and distribute wages," the official said. "You'll make twice what you're earning now, plus free housing, water, electricity and all other living expenses. And you'll be surrounded by water, greenery and fresh air. What do you think?"

81

The custodian did not answer. He tried to imagine himself supervising peasants from Doukkala and Chaouia. He rose to leave, saying he had a train to catch. His cousin said the new job would start on the first of the following month. At that, the custodian's anxiety grew. He forced a smile and hurried out of the house.

The first of the month came and the custodian drove off as usual on his motorcycle, roaring into the traffic which soon swallowed him.

That same day, the official received a cable from his cousin. "I cannot accept your offer," it read, "as it would create difficulties in the children's education. Thank you anyway."

The official exploded in anger. "It's useless trying to help the man! He'll die as miserable as he lived!" His voice lowered. "And these are the men who blame the government for their wretched lives!"

"Some people are born to follow orders and others to give them," his assistant said, unaware that the two men were related.

The official wadded the telegram into a tight ball, then with a flick of his thumb tossed it into a wastebasket.

Divorce

The emaciated young man was suffering long moments of uneasy anticipation; he did not join his colleagues in their usual chat about the issues of the hour. He tapped his pen against his desk, looked at his watch, threw the pen down, crossed his arms and laid his head down on them. Finally, he rose anxiously and left the office. "He's on his way to receive word about his application for promotion," explained one of the men.

A moment later, the emaciated young man returned with a dejected look in his eyes. He sat down and remained at his desk until it was time for him to go home. He walked down the halls, the rhythm of his steps in time with his breathing.

Outside in the street he got on his motorcycle and drove off recklessly, disregarding all traffic signs. He overtook a car from the right and swerved across the road. Moving like an expert roller skater, he attempted to pass a bus from the left, but as the bus came to a turn it blocked his way. He applied his brakes forcefully and was immediately thrown off the motorcycle into the middle of the road. The oncoming car that he had passed a moment earlier came to a sharp stop, its tires shrieking. The young man was bruised and scratched. A hole was torn in the right knee of his trousers as though that spot in his trousers melted in the air. A small crowd of pedestrians collected around him and the driver of the car scolded him. Someone in the crowd helped him to stand up and handed him his motorcycle. At that moment he was overwhelmed with distress. He walked along, pushing his motorcycle on the sidewalk, and broke into sobs.

At home, his wife brought him some cotton and an iodine solution. She went back to the next room to tend to the children. They clung together, motionless, as they did everytime their father came home in a bad mood. He, however, went on rubbing the palm of his hand and his knee with the iodine-soaked cotton. The sting of the solution hurt and he clenched his lips and shut his eyes tightly. He did not utter a sound. He lay on a mattress on the bare floor and silence fell on what seemed to be an empty house.

He lay on his back like a corpse for some time. The evening darkness became more and more overwhelming until his brother walked in and turned on the light. He looked at the injured man's leg and heaved a sigh of relief.

"So what was rumored to be a broken leg is no more than a few scratches on your knee!" he exclaimed. "People exaggerate so much they distort the truth. Why don't you sell that motorcycle?"

There was no reply. Staring into his brother's face, he was able to see how very depressed he was. He remained silent for a while, until his injured brother finally spoke out.

"Life is depressing," he said. "I'm at a loss."

"Why? Are you going to let a small traffic accident destroy you?"

"It had nothing to do with the accident."

"Then what is it?"

"Just life in general."

"And only now you discover that things are bad?"

This question angered the emaciated young man. The veins on his forehead swelled and he shouted, "Of course not! I learned that when father abandoned us."

"There you go again, back to the same old story! We're brothers after all, let's be reasonable. You grew up a long time ago and Father was done with his responsibility for you then."

"Then why did I leave school? Why did I marry a woman whom I found abandoned in the street? I am a failure on every score."

"Did anyone force you?"

"Poverty forced me! You know that well, but you pretend you don't."

Silence fell back onto the house until it was interrupted by the call for the evening prayer. The emaciated young man listened attentively, and his anger dissipated. As soon as the prayer call was over, he spoke more calmly and even affectionately to his brother.

"I remember," he said, "when it used to get so cold in our room at home that I would be unable to fall asleep. But at school in the classroom I would feel the warmth spread all over my body and I would be overcome by sleep. School," he went on as a sad smile appeared on his brother's lips, "what good is school when you're hungry? Do you realize how many times Father was married? Perhaps we'll never know the exact number. Men like him, who produce delinquents, are a curse on our society. They should be banned."

"Your bitterness is too intense," put in the brother.

With a dejected, angry look on his face, the emaciated young man went on recalling. "If it had not been for holidays, we would never have seen the man at all. Remember when he insisted I go and show him who my father was? It was just before the Eid al-adha and we were playing ball as he was bringing home the sacrificial sheep.[1] I kicked the ball hard and it struck him right in the nose. It couldn't have been a better kick if I had tried to aim it at his face. He grabbed my shirt collar," he went on with a nervous laugh, his voice shaking. "He squeezed my neck so tightly that I thought he was going to strangle me. I vividly remember him looking me in the eye and saying 'Take me to see your father, you evil omen. I am not letting go of him until I see the filthy dog who fathered him!' he yelled to the men who rushed to my rescue. 'They are doing such a fine job littering this country's streets with outlaws.' He was humiliated, however, when he heard one of the men shout: 'He's your own son! Let go of him! You are going to kill him!'"

"You always go back to the past, everytime we meet, don't you?" commented his brother. "I think your mind is deteriorating."

"The world is what is deteriorating. What on earth is happening to it?"

The two brothers remained silent for a while and only the regular rhythm of their breathing could be heard.

Then the emaciated young man further recalled, with a smile on his face, "Do you remember the story of the bicycle? I had become so obsessed by the desire to own a bicycle that my mother, bless her soul, was worried about me. She sold everything that was worth anything to buy me that bicycle. I was

---

[1]Feast of sacrifice; one of the major religious holidays in Islam. On the condition that he is able to afford it, each head of the household is required to slaughter a sheep (traditionally) in a sacrifice ritual. The meat is meant to be shared with the poor, who are unable to afford it through the rest of the year.

ready to die of grief if she hadn't bought it for me. Children's happiness is so essential isn't it? And it can be destroyed by a number of things, one of which is divorce. I know that. It marks children with psychological scars that never fade."

"Well, I can't stay much longer. I have to be at work at six in the morning, as you know," said the visiting brother, restlessly looking at his watch. He slammed the door as he left. Silence returned to the house, which once again seemed deserted.

The next morning the emaciated young man woke up and began to shout.

"What a mess this shirt collar is!" he cried. "Is this the shirt that I am supposed to wear to the office? I suppose I should hire someone to press it! Or should I simply go and drown in the ocean?"

His wife stood as motionless as a suspect indicted for a crime. Her children came to her for protection and right before their eyes their father rolled the shirt in his hand and threw it in her face. Her voice climbed over his, as she shouted back.

"Don't you dare assault us anymore with your frustrations over your own failure! Don't make things any worse than they are! Don't add your behavior to everything else—depriving us of food and clothing!... Do you suppose I've not spoken up for so long because I worry about your own well-being? Of course not! My forbearance has been strictly for the children's sake. Otherwise, I'd be happier being somebody's maid!"

"Ah, the children!" he said. "Don't think they are going to save you."

He was flabbergasted by her boldness and taken by surprise that she was as discontented as he was. He was indignant that she was insulting his life-style and the way he treated his family. And because he was humiliated he resolved to discipline her.

But, encouraged by her own rebelliousness, she responded to his threats with another curse that made matters worse.

"You'd rather throw these children into the street, wouldn't you?" she yelled. "Exactly like your father did to you. A family tradition you want to keep, huh?"

"Go on, go on turning them against me," he said. "I know your ways." He started toward the door in disarray, putting on his *djellabah.*

"You'll hear from me!" he shouted as he reached for the door.

He walked away and she followed, still shouting back, "Okay. Okay. Be sure you do your very best and go through with all your plans!" she cried after him.

He rushed out and went straight to the *adil's* office where he found them just opening the office for business. One of the officials ushered him in and insisted that he take a seat, as though he suspected the emaciated young man might change his mind and walk out. The two *adils* sat down at their desks.

"You are here to request a divorce, my son?" one of them inquired.

The emaciated young man nodded. The *adil* prepared to write. "I need names, and the date and place of marriage," he said, and added, "I suppose you know our fees are set."

The emaciated young man sat there reflecting upon these words when the image of a gravedigger flashed through his mind. He was suddenly amazed by the fact that some people live on the calamities of others.

"Names, please, young man. Date and place," the *adil* repeated. He wrote them down as they were given to him and read aloud what he was writing, as if he were dictating it all to himself.

When he finished, the emaciated young man handed him a fifty-dirham[2] note and departed.

---

[2]the equivalent of approximately $6.00

Silence

On the eve of Ramadan, a human deluge inundated the main street of the old city, as if Rabat, chained to its administrative desks and preoccupied with the affairs of the government, had forgotten to prepare itself for the holy month until the crescent moon was already on the horizon.

Two elderly women shuffled against the surge of people. One carried a bundle tucked beneath her arm. The first woman, of medium height, still bore traces of youthful beauty. Relatively robust compared with her companion, she strode ahead of the latter into a side alley and sat down on a doorstep.

The second woman was tall and so thin as to seem emaciated. Ill health had yellowed her complexion and deadened all but her eyes.

They waited on the doorstep in some discomfort until dusk descended and the lights in the market shops came on; then like two turtles, continued their slow procession. Past the door of the great mosque they turned into a narrow alley. The first woman fished in her pocket for a large key, unlocked a green cracked door and gave it a push. The door swung open into darkness and the woman entered, carefully feeling her way until she found the light switch. Lit lamps revealed two rooms, a courtyard paved with tiles and a well on the edge of which fragrant herbs grew in tin cans.

The first woman left the front room immediately, but the second tarried to take stock of the room and its contents. A thin embroidered curtain, an old Turkish rug, carved banquettes, cushions stuffed with wool and encased in velvet, velvet pillows, and two beds opposite each other and raised above all else in the room. She sighed and unexpectedly began to cry. A large photograph in the middle of one wall showed a distinguished looking gentleman wearing a fez. She quickly turned away, completely unsettled, as if the man's face hurt her eyes.

She entered the second room to pray and remained there until the first woman called her for supper.

"We'll eat here," she said tersely, breaking her silence for the first time. The food was brought and silence returned, sharp as a sword's edge. They sat cross-legged at opposite sides of the table, reaching for food but avoiding each other's eyes. When supper was finished, the second woman spoke. "Do not wake me for *suhur*[1]. "

When the trumpet signalled the time for *suhur,* however, the second woman still lay awake in her bed. Call to the dawn prayer followed, the sound diffusing from the great mosque's minaret into the breath of morning. The two elderly women rose to pray, side by side, each making her own plea to God.

"Lord, my sister has no one besides myself," the first robust one prayed. "Grant that I may support her in my house until she dies."

"Lord," the second one, the thin one, implored with the same sincerity and urgency, "I pray by the holy month and by all those who fast on the surface of the earth, do not let me die in her house."

The congenial athmosphere of the month of fasting imbued people's spirits with asceticism and the sweetness of devotion, and quenched their hearts with a kind of joy, as if one were lying in a field on a day in May, the scent of flowers and the blue of the heavens meeting in one's soul, cleansing it of blemishes, making it as pure and light as a breeze wafting toward the heavens.

The second woman, the thin one, took pleasure in the serenity of Ramadan. She took to sitting cross-legged by the well in the open courtyard with its tiles washed and glistening before her. The quiet of the courtyard contrasted with the sharpened voices coming from the street and the neighbouring buildings, with the twitter of the swallows who built their nests on the wooden rafters beneath the tile roof of the house. Sitting there, she would surrender her senses to the calm, intoxicating spring air, relaxing her body and emptying her mind. The swallows swooped down and lit on the tiles, hopping about like tennis balls, slipping in among the cans of watered herbs, their long forked tails dragging behind. Then the first woman would set the table for the evening meal by her sister, and the cannon marking the end of the day's fast would boom from a nearby hill overlooking the sea. Children would cheer in the alley, the call

---

[1] the last meal before dawn during Ramadan, the Islamic month of fasting during the day for Muslims.

to sunset prayer would sound and the street would gradually grow quiet as families gathered to eat together.

The days of Ramadan passed like loops of tightly woven knit fabric gradually unravelling. But the house remained immersed in silence. The first woman had grown increasingly tense. Pressure mounted within her, reaching a climax when one day she let fly a string of curses at the twittering swallows. The second woman bowed her head and sat by the well, her hands resting on her knees. The first woman raged against ingratitude, against people who were not properly appreciative of what was done for them. The second woman raised her head; her colorless complexion seemed to pale even more. After a pause she said as if to herself: "All your life your plans have come to nothing. The whores always win."

The first woman struck out in fury. For a moment, the second woman was afraid her sister might actually hit her, but she suddenly stopped, and returned to her place.

"It was all fate," she said in a strange dead voice.

The second sister felt a renewed vigor. "So close the courts then," she said loudly, slapping her hands on her thin thighs. "Cancel the day of reckoning since everything is predestined to happen anyway."

"Divorce is permitted by law," the first replied in a still deader tone, "and he was going to divorce you even if he hadn't married me."

The second woman's exasperation grew. "You're nothing but a vile animal crawling on its belly," she said, her voice rising.

The first woman continued speaking as if she hadn't heard. "I will fulfill my obligation. When I found out you were ill, I brought you from the hospital. I will support you until you die...in my house. God is forgiving and merciful, after all."

The second woman leapt up, then froze, finally understanding the situation for the first time. When her sister went into the kitchen, she slipped out the door. She stopped in the alley to put on her *djellabah*, then walked quickly away.

It was the eve of the feast, for Ramadan was ending. The main street of the *medina* was clogged with people just as it had been on the night before the beginning of the month of the fast.

The thin sister felt she was destined to cross that street on important occasions.

She walked like a phantom, talking sorrowfully to herself all the time. "So! She wants to purge her sin by having me die in her house?! Then bring out my corpse when people distribute alms for the feast!"

The cannon thundered and people in the street dispersed to their homes to begin the celebration. She heard only the sound of her own footsteps in the empty street. She walked to the bus station and bought a ticket.

On the afternoon of the feast there was a knock on the cracked green door. The first woman opened it to find a telegram being handed to her and a voice reading the name, address and message. "Your sister is dead." She turned away, a strange smile frozen on her face.

Dinner in the Black Market

In the midst of a hectic workday, a visitor came to see the employee. She was a middle-aged woman like the employee, and though she was not beautiful, the great care she had obviously bestowed on her appearance lent her a certain attractiveness. Her imported clothes indicated that she was well-to-do.

"I heard your talk on the radio and recognized your voice," she said as she sat down. "Maybe you don't remember, but we were in high school together."

The employee recognized her and quickly summoned to mind her first impression of the woman. She really wasn't that distinguished. She looked at her face and saw the traces of high-quality makeup. The visitor brushed her hand through her hair revealing glittering rings on her fingers. Her face was like that of a model advertising cosmetics in a Western fashion magazine.

"So what are you doing now?" the employee asked.

"I manage an insurance company," the visitor replied, straightening up and crossing one leg over the other.

The telephone rang, interrupting their conversation. The employee lifted the receiver and spoke with the caller, made an appointment, then hung up and turned towards her visitor.

"A rental agent," the employee explained. "I'm having a hard time finding an apartment."

"Why don't you let me help?" the visitor said, taking the employee by surprise. "I have some vacant apartments."

"So you're also in the real estate business?" the employee asked, perplexed.

The visitor laughed. "No, they're just in some buildings I own."

After setting a time for the employee to see the apartments, the visitor departed.

The two met again on the appointed day and headed for their destination, a massive building housing both apartments and fancy shops.

Soon after, the employee and her husband received an unexpected invitation to dinner from the visitor. On the way to her house, they stopped at a petrol station to buy gas and ask directions. The husband paid and put the change in among the bills in his wallet, then carefully placed the wallet in the inner pocket of his jacket.

The house was of European design, with chimneys and a sloping red tile roof, although in Rabat's climate no such architectural features were necessary. The woman met them at the door. Inside, the house could have passed for a museum of rare art. The hostess invited the husband to take off his jacket as the evening was quite warm. He politely declined, but the woman insisted. "No one else is here but some friends, whom, by the way, I'd like you to drive home." As they started inside, she reached for his jacket and slipped it off his shoulders. "I want you to act as if this were your home."

In the living room they found the hostess' husband with another couple. The employee's husband noticed that both men were, like him, in their shirtsleeves. Soon the air of formality dissipated and the hostess was flitting about like a butterfly aglow with pleasure.

The evening ended and the two couples rode home together. The men dominated the conversation which centered on the charms of their hostess.

"So agile and so efficient."

"Did you notice how she always knew the right thing to say? And what clever jokes she told!"

"It's no wonder she's successful in business."

And so it went, the two men tossing praises back and forth, intoxicated by the evening's mirth, while their wives sat silently in the back seat. The employee's husband took out his cigarettes, only to find the pack empty. He looked to the other man who searched for his pack until he realized he had left it at the woman's house.

"Thank God you didn't forget yourself there," his wife said in an irritated tone.

The employee's husband parked in front of a store to buy cigarettes. But when he took out his wallet, he found all the bills gone.

"Weren't they there when you bought the gas?" his wife asked.

An image flashed before his eyes. The woman insisting he take off his jacket. He froze, speechless.

The other man opened his wallet to pay, but it, too, was empty.

The Stranger

He arrived in Fez late in the evening. He was anxious to get there that night, for although he had waited thirty years he had no patience left to wait until morning.

At the hotel, a sleepy desk clerk opened his passport and read his name. His eyes opened, now wide awake, as if someone had splashed a glass of water in his face.

So people still remember.

After a porter had brought his bags to the room and left, he opened the doors to the balcony and looked out over an Andalusian garden lit by lamps set into the flowerbeds. The lights of the old *medina* flickered beyond the garden walls, just as they had in his dreams. But in those dreams he had looked down on them from a cold, cramped room. The lights had been far away and the ground far below. He could see his mother there, gesturing for him to jump. "I cannot," he would say but the words never reached her.

Some dreams are difficult to separate from reality, and vice versa.

A wind blew light drizzle onto the balcony, wetting his face. He wiped his cheeks with the sleeves of his clerical robe as if brushing away tears. And perhaps there were tears among the droplets of rain on his face. He stepped back into the room and went to bed but lay sleepless.

Events he thought long forgotten came vividly back to mind, as clearly as if the thirty intervening years had never existed.

He saw himself on that day, a young man standing among monks, all of them facing him, moving and chanting. His eyes were fixed on a candelabrum, as tall as the boy who carried it, and he tried to imagine what would happen at home when the news reached them.

His mother would again be struck by the terrifying fits he had witnessed once as a child and which so tormented him he had wished himself dead.

She would beat her face and thighs, uncover her head and pull her hair. She would throw her large body on the ground and go into convulsions like a slaughtered rooster. She would utter cryptic riddles as if someone else inside her was speaking with her tongue. Servants would bring a brazier and burn incense, sprinkle orange-blossom water on her face and bring in the *Imam* of the mosque to exorcise, through the words of the Quran, the spirits afflicting her.

His father would be so completely bewildered he would do nothing. Only later would he realize what had happened.

The news would circulate through town in record speed. Scandals in underdeveloped countries are like farm butter. Even from deep inside the earthen jars, its odor emerges to fill the air.

Lamentations and sorrowful chants of mourning women would smother the house, while the men would say over and over, in sympathy or with resignation, "There is no power nor strength save in God."

Caught up in his daydream, he had not noticed the ritual had ended. They escorted him out of the cathedral and he realized now he was a convert, that his name would be amended to suit a Latin pronunciation, and "Mon Pere" would be added to it. He would have to accustom himself to a new identity.

The next day he learned that an empty coffin had been carried from his house to the cemetery, accompanied by the whole town. The streets thundered with crowds chanting "There is no God but Allah and Mohammed is his messenger" so loudly that some thought that Judgement Day had come.

He read in the colonialist paper published in Rabat that "the policy of accepting Moroccan children into Christian schools had born its first fruit." Further down, however, the story warned that the event might sow fear in the populace and make them wary of allowing their children a French education.

So ended his ties with family and city. He was next sent to France where he began his new life in a monastic order and pursued his studies.

He felt a twinge in his arm as he usually did whenever he slept on his right side. He sat up in bed and switched on the light, then called the desk clerk to ask the time.

"Three A.M."

He adjusted his watch which was still set on French time, turned the light off and stared into darkness. More images came back to his mind.

He is five years old. His father is beating his mother as he cries and screams and nearly dies from terror. He grabs the hem of his mother's skirt as she is pulling at his father's collar, and the three of them drag themselves around a marble fountain in the middle of the mosaic-tiled courtyard. Words are lost amidst screams and wails. He understands only disconnected phrases: "marriage," "second wife," "black maid."

That was the day he first saw his mother convulse in an epileptic fit. That was the year he entered the monk's school as a student.

The boy who did odd jobs around the house used to carry him to and from school on his shoulders. He had paid the boy with sweets bought at the mausoleum of Moulay Idris. The Moroccan children would pay for the sweets with the spools of wool Sister Régine had given them at the school for that purpose.

He would chew on the hard white candy, his mouth watering, and from his vantage point above the boy's skull cap, he watched the passing shops and craftsmen. He kept his fingers hooked around that cap as the boy held firmly on his ankles to keep him from slipping.

At home Yasmine would greet him with great fanfare. She had raised him from birth and loved him as if he were her own son. She was forever telling him the story of how she had arrived from Senegal, how slave traders had stolen her as a child and sold her. He would listen in rapt attention, studying her deep black face and flashing white teeth.

He loved to climb on her back when she knelt to pray. If his mother caught him and tried to beat him, Yasmine would intervene. She was always like that, always his ally and protector, right or wrong, and would become very angry if his father punished him.

He wondered how Yasmine looked now.

Roosters began crowing on nearby roofs, and the voice of the *muezzin* bellowed. Without realizing it, he was finally overcome by sleep.

He woke at eight and left the hotel without taking breakfast. He soon found himself in rainwashed alleys, his breast filled with unexpected delight. He inhaled, a deep breath of chill morning air mixed with the scent of fresh mint being sold in bunches by a man on the sidewalk.

He walked, hungry to take in the city, his eyes yearning to see as much as possible, his senses reaching out to the stone-paved alleys and streets, the worn walls, the clopping mules that had carried men and goods through the streets of Fez for more than a thousand years.

As the morning progressed, stores and workshops began opening and the sound of hammers striking on metal echoed in the streets.

Everything was the same, as though time in this city had stopped.

Joy flowed into his soul from all he saw and he felt a burst of affection for the people around him. Men he thought, like trees, are rooted in the land.

He spied a face resembling that of his father and he stopped dead in the middle of the street, his heart pounding. "Balaak!" a mule-driver shouted, rousing him from his trance. He pressed against a wall so that the mule loaded with tanned skins could pass. The reek of the skins filled his nostrils. He had never understood the meaning of "balaak," stressing the first syllable to warn people to pay attention.

He came to the mosque near the narrow street where he had lived. At its door, as always, a group of blind men recited the Quran in their Moroccan accents. Again his heart pounded.

He headed for the house and found its door ajar. He lightly rapped the iron hand that served as a knocker. As a child he had shown no mercy to this door, kicking and banging until someone opened it. After a moment he heard heavy footsteps and bracelets jangling. Yasmine's face peered from behind the door. Though she had aged, he still recognized her. Gazing at her face, he could no longer conjure up his earlier images of her.

She recognized him as well but said nothing. From inside the house came the voice of an elderly woman. His mother most likely. "Who is it?" she asked.

Old Yasmine disappeared for what seemed a long time. When she returned he said to her, "I am Aziz... Don't you recognize me?"

"Aziz is dead," she said dryly. "We buried him thirty years ago." She shut the door and he heard her footsteps retreating.

He looked around, sensing eyes watching him. He tried to walk but found his legs heavy and numb. He wished that taxis ventured into these alleys.

Eventually he sat down in an orange-juice bar by the mosque, and heard the waiter speak as he sat a glass before him.

"Depressing weather today."

His spirit was equally gloomy. Sunk in sadness, he had no idea how long he sat there. When he left, he again passed the group of blind beggars. Their mournful chanting trailed him until he disappeared from view.

Out of Work

When I lost my job in 1980, after seven years in the same position, I had been working a full decade. During that time I drove my car between home and work six days a week, four times a day except Saturdays. I drove the route without even thinking, responding to traffic lights with automatic reflexes that rarely failed. If someone had asked me what kinds of trees grew along the road I could not have told them, save for the palms lining the main avenue, which led to the street where our house was. I knew the palms for sure because I used them as a landmark when directing visitors to our address.

In the beginning driving was easy; with fewer cars in the streets I could look left and right. Now I could hardly get home safely through the heavy traffic with cars passing on all sides, even overhead it seemed, and pedestrians charging across streets at times and places impossible to predict.

When I was preparing for my driving exam, the instructor told me, "Behind the wheel you are actually driving three cars." Why not include motorcycles and pedestrians as well?

After buying my car, I lost contact with the people who live in the neighborhood. Contractors bought most of the single-story houses with gardens and trees and flattened them to build modern apartment buildings in their place; young couples with big incomes lived in those apartments. The original residents whom I had come to know as a student when I traveled around by foot had all moved elsewhere.

After losing my job, however, I began walking again, using the opportunity to explore the neighborhood and city. For the first time I saw how few single-story houses remained, their trellised hedges blooming with bougainvillaea, hibiscus and geraniums. Most of those shrubs now were overgrown, flowing onto sidewalks and actually invading the houses themselves. Only one still had a gardener who watered the garden and washed the front sidewalk every day before sunset. He neatly pruned the bushes so that a white rose crowned the leafy hedges surrounding the house.

Shops had sprung up alongside the apartment buildings. Polished brass plaques announced the names of offices and clinics. Other signs in Arabic and French, some rudimentary and some quite sophisticated, hung over refrigerator repair shops, bakeries, photography studios, pharmacies, bookshops, beauty salons, banks, and show windows displaying boxes, perfume bottles, and colored combs. More apartment buildings were being built; the quiet neighborhood was changing into a booming commercial center.

I found its main street and square crowded with new faces. The clothes worn by the young girls represented serious financial investments, and their coiffures demonstrated both effort and creativity. The efforts at fashion by young married women were not up to the single girls'; glimpsed from behind car windshields, the faces of couples reflected their bad moods. I bet to myself that I would not find two people smiling in the same car. I won.

After roaming through my old neighborhood I extended my exploration into the city. I returned to the narrow streets of the old part of town, the *medina*, and took time to appreciate it, redolant with the scent of the past. I headed east, north and south, stumbling on from poor quarters to luxurious ones, finding markets I never knew existed, and secret, scary squatter settlements purposefully concealed from view.

Now that I was out of work, I could stop and look at my leisure. Nothing to do and plenty of time, all the time in the world to discover the city I had lived in for twenty years.

Glossary

adil: chartered judicial officials possessing enough knowledge of Islamic law to be able to witness and endorse marriage, divorce and inheritance proceedings

caid: a local administrator, judge and tax collector

dhikr: in Sufism, the incessant repetition of God's praises, often accompanied by music and dancing

djellabah: a full loose garment with a hood and with sleeves and skirt of varying length

faqih: in popular usage, a religious specialist

fidai: a guerilla fighter in the resistance

fidaiyiin: plural of fidai

foundouk: a two-storied structure with rooms on the second floor opening onto a veranda

harira: Moroccan soup

imam: religious leader/ prayer leader

inshallah: "If God is willing," a frequently used expression among Muslims

jihad: a bitter strife or crusade undertaken in the spirit of a holy war

kif: a smoking material (as Indian hemp) that produces a state of dreamy tranquility

medina: literally "city"; in North Africa, refers to the native quarter of a North African city

mihrab: the niche in the Mosque wall indicating the direction of Mecca

mizmar: a pipe instrument

muezzin: a Muslim crier that cries the hour of daily prayer from the minaret of a mosque

pasha: a man of high rank or office

rakaa: part of the Muslim prayer ritual

sheikh: a Muslim religious leader or scholar

Modern Middle East Literature

in

Translation

Series

By the Pen by Jalal Al-Ahmad

Year of the Elephant by Leila Abouzeid

Istanbul Boy, Parts I and II by Aziz Nesin

Forthcoming

> *Fragments of Memory* by Hanna Mina
>
> *Portrait of Damascus* by Siham Tergeman
>
> *Since the Iranian Revolution, Stories by Persian Women* edited by Soraya Sullivan
>
> *That's All That's Left to You* by Ghassan Kanafani
>
> (Published by the Center for Middle Eastern Studies and distributed by the University of Texas Press)